MARIO'S NOTEBOOK

Mary Atkinson

Cover illustration by Elizabeth Gomez
www.elizabethgomezart.com

ISBN: 1983745871
ISBN 13: 9781983745874
Library of Congress Control Number: 2018901688
CreateSpace Independent Publishing Platform
North Charleston, South Carolina

For all the people of El Salvador

1

My first wish is that Señor Perez would turn off the opera on the car radio. My second wish is that he'd stop smoking his cigar. It's disgusting the way he chews on it and rolls it from one side of his mouth to the other. I can't breathe and it smells like horse manure in here. My third wish is that my little brother Nico would stop bouncing around on the back seat and we could get out of this stupid car and walk home from school like we used to.

Ya lo sé. I know. My country is at war. Mamá has told me a million times that she feels better if we ride with our gardener instead of walking. Especially since Archbishop Romero was killed just three days ago.

Of course my real wish is to stop the war. If I had super powers, that's what I'd do. But I'm only a ten-year-old kid, and I'm stuck in this smoky car right now with the windows closed and some lady is singing on the radio like she's got a cat in her throat and it's scratching my ears out!

"Hurry up, get out of the street," Señor Perez grumbles to the people outside our air-conditioned car. He's pressing on the horn, honking at cars and people to get out of the way. "Move along, *imbécil*!" he calls. If Mamá could hear the way he swears, maybe then she'd think twice about asking him to drive us home from school.

A broken-down bus blocks the intersection in a plaza not far from our house. Three men are hanging out the windows, banging their arms, slapping the bus like they're trying to get it moving again.

"Hey, Mario, catch!" Nico says. He tosses me his new soccer ball. Papá just gave it to him for his fifth birthday. Nico doesn't go anywhere without it. He even sleeps with that ball! We play catch in the back seat.

"Damn traffic," Señor Perez says. "And me with a thirst like a man in the dessert."

Señor Perez is thirsty? Uh-oh. I'm getting an idea. A voice pops into my head: *Mario, do you really think you should go through with this?* I should but I don't listen.

To my better self, Papá would say.

"*Perdón*, Señor Perez," I say. "See that café right across the street? This traffic's not going anywhere. You could pull over and get yourself a drink."

The señor eyes the café. It has a torn blue awning. Through the opened door we see people sipping on tall drinks or from little cups of coffee. All around the plaza, the traffic is stalled. Drivers are honking and yelling and waving their arms in the air, but nothing moves. Two government soldiers stand on the corner, their shiny black hats tilted against the setting sun.

"You're right, Mario. It's going to take them all afternoon to clean up this mess," Señor Perez says. He angles the car to the curb and opens his door. Smoke pours out. "Now listen, you two. Don't move. Stay in the car," he tells us. "I'll be right back."

Nico and I watch as Señor Perez makes his way through the square. At the outdoor market, *indígenas* from the mountains hang woven blankets and clothing on racks to sell. Farmers set out large baskets overflowing with fruits and vegetables. Braids of onions and garlic drape over one farmer's shoulders. He walks along the street, calling out, "*Cebollas. Ajos. Tengo cebollas. Ajos,*" asking people if they want to buy some.

Señor Perez goes into the café. That's when I open my door and nudge Nico. "*Vamos,*" I say.

"But Señor Perez said…." Nico's eyes are wide. He's already grabbing his soccer ball and sliding to my side of the car.

Nico never worries about my better self.

We tumble out of the car while Señor Perez gets his *refresco.* At last we are freed from Señor Perez's smoky cage, and Nico wants to play. He throws his black and white soccer ball into the road. We're standing next to the car, kicking the ball back and forth. "Step back,

Nico," I say. "Get ready for this one!" I tap the ball with the inside of my foot.

We widen the space and keep dribbling. Lively radio music from *charangos*, flutes, and drums pours out the open doors and windows of the tailor's shop. Inside, I see a man at a sewing machine and a woman ironing. The smell of frying plantains coming from a vendor's cart makes my stomach growl. I'm thinking maybe there's time to run down the street and get some before Señor Perez comes back when Nico yells, "Mario! My ball!"

Nico has kicked the ball too hard and it's rolling in the gutter down a hill away from the plaza. "Come on. Let's get it!" I say, chasing after the ball. Nico follows.

We run a down a side street. Up ahead is a man staring under the hood of a car. At his feet he's got a cardboard box stained with grease and filled with tools. He's scratching his head. I like how he looks like that, bent over and thinking what to do. I fix the picture in my mind to draw later.

Finally, I reach the ball and stop it with my foot. I'm catching my breath when Nico charges from behind and kicks it out from under me. "Oh, great, Nico," I say. It's a good, strong kick for a five-year-old – too strong and going in the wrong direction. Señor Perez is probably leaving the café right now. Nico's high kick lands the ball – splash! – in a muddy puddle left by an afternoon shower. It bounces against a man's legs and rests at his feet.

My stomach sinks. Nico's target is a soldier.

2

OUT OF PLACE

The soldier looks down at his creased pant legs and black boots splattered with mud. Then he glares at us and scowls. He has a young face, like the teenagers in the upper grades at our school. A rifle dangles from his shoulder. Next to Scowly-Face is another soldier, smoking a cigarette. They're standing with two girls. The girls look like teenagers, too, with bright lipstick, hair pulled back, and hoop earrings. Papá has told me to stay away from the soldiers patrolling the streets now in San Salvador.

Scowly-Face pokes me in the arm with the butt of his rifle. "What do you two think you're doing in this *colonia*?" he asks. He kicks the water in the puddle. It splashes my bare legs. "You wouldn't want to get those nice uniforms all muddy, would you?" Suddenly, I'm aware of our blue shorts and white shirts with the emblem from the private school we go to. Across the street some boys in ragged clothes are playing a game, tossing pebbles into empty tin cans. Papá says there are children in El Salvador who don't even go to school.

Scowly-Face widens his stance and crosses his rifle across his chest. One of the girls fiddles with her bracelets. They jangle and clatter like a rattlesnake's tail.

How could I be so stupid? Playing soccer in the streets of San Salvador like everything is normal? Like there's no war going on? I'm the older brother. Mamá wants me to watch out for Nico, not put him in danger. I stand up straight. "We're sorry. We didn't mean…" I say.

"They're sor-ry, Jorge," Scowly-Face interrupts, mimicking me.

The girls giggle.

"What's your name?" Jorge asks.

"Mario," I squeak.

"Speak up, boy. Mario what?"

"Zamora. Mario Zamora is my name." I try to keep my voice steady, but it feels like a bus about ready to swerve off a cliff.

"And you?" Scowly-Face turns to Nico.

Nico looks to me and says nothing. "He's my little brother," I answer for him. "His name is Nico."

"And where are the two brothers going?" Jorge asks.

"*A casa*, señores," I say. "We're going home."

"Around here? Surely you don't live around here," Scowly-Face says. He gestures to the neighborhood of rundown buildings, paint peeling off doors, holes in stucco walls, broken windows held together by tape, trash in the streets. A skinny black dog slinks under a fence and disappears.

"A traffic jam. Up there. In the plaza. We got out. The ball…" I'm sputtering. The bus is careening off the road.

Just then Nico's soccer ball starts rolling down the street. Nico makes a move to go after it. I grab his shoulders and hold him back.

With his boot, Scowly-Face slams down on the ball. "Nice soccer ball, eh, Jorge?" he asks. He picks up the ball and spins it around on the tip of his finger.

"Very nice. I wouldn't mind having me a soccer ball like that," Jorge says.

"Then take it." Scowly-Face throws the ball to his friend.

"But it's mine! I just got it for my birthday," Nico says.

Shut up, Nico. Shut up!

"For his birthday, Jorge. Now, isn't that sweet," Scowly-Face says.

"Poor baby Nico. Ask your papi to buy you another one." Jorge turns the soccer ball in his hand. He spits his cigarette to the ground and leaves it smoldering. "Look here, *bichos*," he says, narrowing his eyes. "Look what happens to little boys who run the streets in the wrong part of town." Jorge's black, glassy eyes glisten and grow wide. Laughing, he pulls a knife from his belt. It's a big knife, like the one *Abuelo* uses when he goes hunting. The blade catches the light as Jorge turns it in his hand. Quickly, he jabs the knife into the ball. The ball makes a slow hissing sound.

"My ball!" Nico cries out.

Jorge lifts the skewered ball into the air. Raspy laughter peels from his throat. The girls are watching. Their jewelry doesn't clink. Their giggling has stopped. They don't say a word.

I gasp and clamp my hand over my mouth. Nico's fingers hang on to my arm like claws.

"Oh, get lost, *señoritas*," the soldier says. "Go home to your mami and papi." He waves us off. He throws the punctured ball to the ground and kicks it into the gutter.

I pry Nico's fingers from my arm. I take his hand and pull him to follow me. "Run!" I say. We hurry back up the hill to the town square.

"That's right, little Mamá's boys. Better run fast. Fast as you can!" Scowley-Face yells. He lunges after us then stops short, but his laughter follows like a round of bullets shooting from his rifle.

We make it back to Señor Perez's car just as he's leaving the café. I open the door and push Nico into the back seat. We're sweaty and out of breath. Nico begins to cry. "Don't cry, Nico," I say. I use my school shirttails to wipe his cheeks.

Nico keeps sniffling.

"Look. Señor Perez is coming. He can't know. Just hold your breath and stop crying," I say.

Nico gulps air. "What about my ball?" he asks.

"Your ball? Is that all you care about?"

Nico kicks his heels against the seat. "Why were those soldiers so mean to us, Mario?" he asks.

"I don't know," I answer. Nico expects me to have all the answers, just because I'm the older brother. My breathing has quieted, but I still feel like I can't get enough air. Mamá said there were soldiers in the city now to protect the people, but I don't feel protected. I feel attacked.

"Ready, boys?" Señor Perez gets in the car. The cigar is gone. His breath smells like alcohol now. People have pushed the bus out of the intersection and the traffic is beginning to move. "Fine idea you had there, Mario. I feel like a new man!" He starts up the engine and turns the radio back on.

I press my cheek to the closed window and wait for the car air to cool. I don't care what's on the radio anymore. Nico slides over to sit right next to me. I don't push him away.

3

LOS NERVIOS DE MAMÁ

Señor Perez stops the car to open the gates to our house. Nico and I jump out and run up our pebble driveway. The señor pulls the car in and locks the gates behind us. Nico and I walk to the back of the house where the kitchen opens onto a patio surrounded by green leafy plants with red, purple, and pink flowers in big clay pots. Mamá's canaries sing in their bamboo cage. Blanca, our maid, is waiting for us in the kitchen. Papá is still teaching at the university, and Mamá isn't home yet from her job at the bank.

"How about a nice cold glass of *horchata*?" Blanca asks. She puts two glasses of the sweet rice drink on the kitchen table. "You're late today. What took so long?"

Nico and I both answer at once. "Soldiers," he says. "Traffic jam," I say.

"Soldiers? What soldiers? Weren't you with Señor Perez?" she asks.

"They took my soccer ball," Nico says.

"Nico." I glare at him. "Let me explain." I tell Blanca about the traffic jam, how we got out of the car when Señor Perez stopped for a drink, and how we had to chase Nico's ball. "The soldiers were just playing around with us, Blanca," I say. "It was no big deal." I don't tell her what they did to the ball.

"You should be careful, Mario," Blanca says. "After what happened to Archbishop Romero, the whole city is on edge. I worry for the people of my *pueblo*. The *policía*, the soldiers – everyone's acting crazy now. They bother innocent people, people who have nothing to do with the war. *Ay*, Mario, what am I saying?" Blanca's eyes dart around the kitchen. She closes the patio doors and turns on some music. "No more talk of soldiers now. Not with this plump chicken I have to cut up for dinner."

Blanca spreads the chicken on a cutting board. With a kitchen knife she whacks it into small pieces for frying.

"The soldiers had a big knife, too," Nico says.

"What?" Blanca asks.

"Nico's talking about a knife one of the soldiers carried in his belt. That's all," I say.

"Forget about those soldiers, Nico," Blanca says. "And say nothing to your mamá. Already she worries too much. It's bad for her *nervios*."

That night Mamá and Papá come home late. Blanca has given Nico his bath and put him to bed. I am still up, drawing in my notebook at my desk. I love to draw. When I grow up, I want to be an artist.

I start out trying to draw the man I saw today looking under the hood of the car, but the questioning expression on his face turns into a scowl, his wrench into a rifle, and his pants and shirt into the soldier's uniform. Now a soldier stares at me from the paper. I turn the page and start over.

I hear Mamá and Papá arguing as they enter the house. Blanca was right about Mamá's *nervios*. It doesn't take much lately to upset her. I choose a blue pencil for the old man's car.

"I don't see why *you* have to write all the articles," Mamá is saying to Papá. "Can't you get one of your students to do it for once? What about Oscar? He's a good writer."

"Of course, he can," Papá says. "But it's my name people look for in the paper."

"That's just it! Too many people recognize your name!" Mamá cries.

What's wrong with people knowing Papá's name? I put the pencil away, close my pad, and stretch my ears to listen.

"*Ay,* Joaquín, *por favor,* couldn't you lay low for a while? We could take the boys to my father's *finca.* We'd be safer there," Mamá says.

I tiptoe out of my room. I can see Mamá and Papá at the end of the hall. Their bodies are dark silhouettes in the dimly lit entrance to our house.

"And what would you have me do, María Elena?" Papá asks. "Stop writing? Sit back while our people kill each other and do nothing?"

"*Ay*, no. Of course not. It's just that sometimes," Mamá says, "sometimes I get so scared."

Papá puts down his briefcase and wraps his arms around Mamá. She cries softly onto his shoulder. I creep back into my room and sit at my desk. I don't know which scares me more: the soldiers, the war, or seeing Mamá cry.

Mamá stops by my room. There are black smudges under her eyes where the make-up has run. She sits on my bed, as she usually does, and asks me how was my day, have I done my homework, did Blanca cook a nice dinner?

"I have an English quiz tomorrow," I say. "Can you test me?" I hand her the book.

"What page are we on?" she asks.

"Seventy-three. I have to know all the irregular verbs in that list." As Mamá finds the page, I'm thinking about what Blanca said about Mamá's nerves. I'm going to pretend this is just another regular night of homework, even though inside I can't shake the picture of the soldier's knife piercing through Nico's soccer ball.

"Ring," Mamá says the first verb.

"Ring, rang, rung," I say.

"Go," Mamá says.

"Go, went, gone."

"*Muy bien, mijo.*" Mamá says. "Run."

"Run, ran, run."

Mamá finishes the list of verbs. When we're done, she says, "Go tell Papá. Tell him you got them all right."

4

PAPÁ'S WORDS

I take the book and go to the living room. All the windows in our house are closed and the drapes are drawn. Ever since the curfew, we keep the house dark. Our street is quiet at night. I don't hear cars pass by or music coming though our neighbors' opened windows. Sometimes planes scream overhead and I hear the sounds of bombing in the distance. And always, the sound of Papá's steady typing.

Tonight, Papá's typing has stopped. Crumpled balls of paper dot the floor. Papá's hunched over a blank sheet of paper, pulling his hands through his thick, messy hair. "Papá?" I say quietly. I'm not supposed to interrupt him if he's thinking.

Papá's eyes brighten when he sees me. I want to tell him everything – about the traffic jam, the soldiers, Nico's ball.

"Mamá wants you to hear my English verbs," I say.

"You've learned them?" he asks.

"Yes, Papá. I know them all."

"Those English verbs sure are tricky. I could never get all the –*eds* and the –*ings*." Papá stands up and hugs me. He smells of coffee and black tobacco and his hug makes me feel safe and warm. "Knowing English is so important for our future. Give me your book. Let's practice some more." Papá flips through the pages until he finds another list.

"Papá?" I say.

"What is it, *mijo*? Tired of studying?" Papá asks.

"No, it's not that." I take a breath. I can't keep it inside anymore. I have to tell him. "Two soldiers stopped me and Nico. On the way home from school."

"And Señor Perez?" Papá asks.

I shake my head. "He wasn't with us. We were stuck in traffic. He went to get a drink." The words spill out as I tell Papá the whole story, how it was my idea to get out of the car, how Nico's ball ran down the hill and splashed in a puddle against a soldier's legs. I leave out the part about how it was me who suggested the drink to Sr. Perez in the first place. Papá doesn't like to hear about me causing mischief. "I'm sorry, Papá. It was all my fault."

Papá paces back and forth. "These soldiers, did they ask for your names?" he asks.

I remember what Mamá said about too many people knowing Papá's name. "No, Papá," I lie. "But they, they took Nico's soccer ball and one of them had a knife and he... He was playing around with the ball, and then, well, he stabbed it with the knife."

"They threatened you like that?" Papá asks.

"They were laughing at us. They thought it was funny," I say. "But why, Papá? Why do they have to bother us like that? We're only kids. We have nothing to do with the war. Why does there even have to be a war?"

Papá sinks down in his chair. "Dear god, what is happening to our country?" he says. "Soldiers picking on children now? What next?" He signals for me to sit on his lap. His arms feel good wrapped around me.

"I'm glad you told me what happened, Mario," Papá says. "These soldiers, they're just kids themselves. They're recruited from poor families in the countryside. They don't know what they're doing. But messing around with children? Doesn't anyone understand what this war is doing to our people?"

Papá looks me in the eyes. "From now on," he says. "I want you to stay in Señor Perez's car. Come straight home from school. And talk to no one on the streets. *¿Comprendes?*"

"Yes, Papá," I say. "I understand."

"You're a good boy to talk to me," Papá says. "Are you all right?"

I nod.

"Well then, I'd better get back to work. They need my piece first thing in the morning."

"What are you writing about this week?" I ask, getting off his lap.

"I don't know yet, *mijo*," Papá says, shaking his head. He squeezes my shoulder and goes his desk. Papá's eyes go back into himself, the way they always do when he's thinking, and soon he's lost in his own world of words.

I go back to my room and get into bed. I don't get it. I don't understand why our country has to be at war. Everybody loved Archbishop Romero, but he was murdered. Guerillas shot and killed a professor at Papá's university. And last week, one of Mamá's friends came over. She was sobbing to Mamá. Her husband, a doctor at a clinic for poor people, was taken away by government soldiers in a van. He's been missing for over a month. Papá says there are people on both sides who aren't happy with the ways things are going in our country. But why do they have to kill? Why can't they just talk to each other?

I'm trying to fall asleep, but I keep imagining a man like Scowly-Face, lifting his rifle, taking aim, and firing. In my head I see a priest, crumbling to the floor, his black robes soaked in blood. I see the professor, surprised by the intruder in his office, throwing his arms in the air. Then I see his body slumped over papers on his desk, splattered with blood.

I shake these horrible pictures from my head. Instead, I make myself think of Abuelo's farm. I turn on the light and reach for my notebook. I make a rough outline of the mountains behind Abuelo's house. I plant some palm trees. With my green pencils I make sure no two fronds look alike. I add tiny lines on the tree trunks to show the rough bark. The drawing calms me down. Soon I feel drowsy.

Mamá comes into my room. "Your light's still on? It's way past time for bed," she says.

I hold up my picture. "Like it so far?" I ask.

"*Ay, sí*, Mario. You know I always like your drawings, but even an artist needs his sleep."

"Are we going to Abuelo's on Sunday?" I ask.

"On Sunday, as usual," she says, kissing me good-night. She tucks me in and pulls the covers close.

I love getting out of the city and going to Abuelo's farm. I shut my eyes and force images of the farm through my head like a movie: rugged hills dotted with coffee trees, low clouds in a deep blue sky, jagged mountains in the distance, donkeys carrying baskets of beans, horses flicking their tails, birds flying overhead. Abuelo says El Salvador is the most beautiful country in the world. The soldier, the priest and the professor fade away. I can't wait until Sunday. There will be no end to the drawings I can make at Abuelo's farm.

5

SHATTERING GLASS

Clomp, clomp, clomp! A loud noise wakes me in the middle of the night. Clomp, clomp, clomp, clomp, CLOMP! I sit up and wipe the sleep from my eyes. My clock says 3:00 a.m. Craaash! What was that? Glass breaking? A window? A lamp? Am I dreaming? Furniture scrapes across the floor.

"No!" Mamá wails. "No, *por favor*. Not Joaquín. Not my Joaquín. I beg you. Please!"

I jump out of bed, open my door, and look out. Three soldiers surround Papá. He's wearing his pajamas. Bandannas cover their faces. Are those Scowly-Face's beady eyes poking out from one?

"Not my Joaquín. *Por favor*, have mercy. My husband, he is a teacher. He has done nothing!" Mamá yells.

I step into the hall. What's going on? Why are these soldiers here? I've heard about soldiers coming at night, stealing people away. But not Papá. Not Papá! I have to stop them.

I sneak down the hall. Papá sees me. In the harsh light, he glares at me. It's as if his eyes are about to reach over and grab me. They flit to one side. Is Papá giving me a signal?

Yes! To the typewriter. My heart is thumping like a stick banging a drum. Too loud? Can the soldiers hear it, too? I creep along the wall's edge. At Papá's desk, I slowly and quietly pull the sheet of paper from his typewriter. Papá nods. The paper shakes in my trembling hands. Papá bends his head in the direction of my room. "Go," his stern eyes tell me.

One soldier is tying Papá's arms behind his back. Another is rummaging through Papá's papers, throwing his books to the floor. Not his dictionary! Not his books of poetry! Papá loves his books of poetry. I rush into the hall, ready to jump the soldiers, pull them off Papá, kick them, bite them, hit them with a lamp, anything. But Papá is shaking his head, no, as if he can read my mind. Mamá sees me, too. She moves to stand between me and the soldiers. She waves her hands behind her back. "Go to your room," her hands say. "Stay away."

I chew on the inside of my cheek until I taste blood. All I can do is watch. Watch as the soldiers blindfold Papá. Watch as they shove him out the door. Watch as Mamá collapses to the floor.

6

OUT OF ORDER

"Mamá!" I cry. I rush to her side. She is lying on the floor, her black hair spilled out in spikes all around her head. "Are you all right?" I shake her. "Mamá, wake up! Where are they taking Papá?"

Slowly, Mamá opens her eyes. She brushes the hair from her face. She looks like she's trying to figure out who I am. Her eyes widen. Then she jumps up like someone has thrown cold water in her face. "Tío Nicolás," she says in a hoarse voice. She stumbles to the telephone. "Go check on Nico. Make sure he's all right."

I run to a window and look out. In the night, a van disappears around the corner. "Papá?" I call, pressing my hand to the glass. "Papá!" Where is the van taking him?

I look around the room. Papá's papers are strewn everywhere. Papá hates his papers out of order. He doesn't let anyone touch the piles on his desk. And now they're all over the place – under the desk, on his chair, scattered over the rug. I start picking them up, squaring them off in the neat piles he likes.

"Mario, leave those now!" Mamá yells. "Get Nico, I said."

I drift into Nico's room. These can't be my feet that are carrying me. They must belong to someone else. My head doesn't feel attached to my body. Nico's sleeping with his toys, as usual – two story books, his stuffed bear, and *Rana,* the wooden frog Papá gave for him on his birthday for good luck. His face is peaceful. His breathing makes a soft sound. He smells clean, like soap. "Wake up, Nico," I whisper.

"Huh?" Nico says, rubbing his eyes. "Is it time for breakfast?"

"No. Not breakfast. It's nighttime. Papá's gone."

"Papá? Gone?" Nico looks around the room.

Why did I have to say that? "Don't worry. He'll be back soon, I think. The soldiers just wanted to ask him some questions."

"Soldiers?" Nico hops out of bed. He stares up at me, his eyes bright. Am I crazy? What am I doing, talking to Nico about Papá gone and soldiers? He pushes past me. I can't stop him. He's running to Mamá. He practically jumps into her arms. She lifts him up.

Tío Nicolás bursts through the front door. Mamá sees him and starts sobbing. "They took my Joaquín. My Joaquín, he's gone."

"You must grab your things and go at once, just like we planned," Nicolás says.

"Go?" I ask. "In the middle of the night? Where?"

"María Elena," Nicolás interrupts. He hands Mamá a cloth pouch with a long strap. "Wear this around your neck and crossed under your arm. Keep it on you at all times. Inside are your bus tickets and money and addresses of people who will help along the way."

"Tickets?" I ask. "For Papá, too?"

"Mario, get your things," Tío Nicolás orders.

"But Tío. Leave now? Why?" I ask.

"It's no longer safe for you here," Nicolás says, his voice hard.

"But what about Papá? Where is he? When are we coming back?" I can't catch my breath.

"Mario, listen to me," Nicolás says. "Get dressed and fill your bag with clothes. Help your brother. There isn't a moment to waste."

The way Tío Nicolás is talking scares me. He's my favorite uncle. Usually he's a lot of fun. Now he sounds so mean. "Nico, do what Tío says," I say. I go to my room and pull on pants and a shirt. The paper from Papá's typewriter is on the floor. I pick it up and stash it in my bag with some clothes.

"Hurry!" Mamá calls.

I sweep up the small toys from my night table and grab my tin of colored pencils. I'm stuffing my notebook in the bag when Nicolás comes into the room. He's carrying Nico and Nico's bag. Nico clutches Rana and his stuffed bear. "The car is waiting. Let's go!"

"Wait," I say. Papá's typewriter is uncovered. I go to his desk to put on its plastic cover. When Papá comes home, he'll get mad if he finds typewriter filled with dust.

A car is waiting out front with its headlights turned off. A black stocking cap covers the driver's face. Someone else is sitting up front, huddled under a blanket. Nicolás opens the back door. I get in first, then Nico, then Mamá. Nico begins to whimper. "Keep him quiet," the driver says. Mamá cups her hand over Nico's mouth. "Hold your breath," I whisper.

"*Vayan con Díos,*" Tío Nicolás says. Go with God. He disappears into the night. We don't even get to say good-bye.

"Mamá, where are we going?" I whisper.

"To the border."

"With Honduras?"

"No, Guatemala."

"We're going to Guatemala?" I ask.

"Then to Mexico. Then *Estados Unidos*," Mamá says.

"But that's so far," I say.

"Hush, *mi cielo.* Get some rest," Mamá says.

"But when can I see Papá?" I ask.

Mamá wraps an arm around me and pulls me close. "Sleep now, *mijo,*" she whispers. "Please sleep."

I'm cuddled next to Mamá, looking out the window. I'm looking for the van that took Papá, but the streets are empty. Only a stray cat runs out of the car's way. Soon the city streets give way to dirt roads. There is only darkness and a black sky full of stars, pinpricks in the night. My eyes grow heavy as the car bounces and rattles me further and further away from home.

7

RADIO CLANDESTINO

"*Radio Clandestino. Buenos días, compas.*" Scratchy sounds from a radio wake me up. "*Veintiocho de marzo, 1980.*" March 28, 1980, I hear the date and open my eyes. The sun is just rising over a small town square. In the shadows a man is bent over a broom, sweeping the sidewalk in front of a small church. Another man unloads bags of potatoes from a wooden cart. Nico is still sleeping, draped over me in the back seat of a car. What are we doing in this car? Where are we? Suddenly, in a blast, everything that happened last night comes back to me. I gently ease the sleeping Nico off of me and sit up.

Up front, the driver's cap is off. He's a young man with curly black hair and a beard. He hands me a bag of candy. "For later," he says. "For you and your brother." Next to him is someone I know. Oscar, one of Papá's students. He's been to our house many times before. The driver speaks to Mamá. "Oscar will accompany you on your trip," he's saying. "Listen carefully. I leave you here in Guijo. Another driver will take you to the border. A man named Rafael will meet you there. Then…"

"Quiet, listen to this," Oscar interrupts. "On the radio." He turns up the volume.

"*¡Boletín!* Special bulletin! Contacts in San Salvador report a sweep through the *Colonia Vigil*," the announcer says.

"Mamá, that's our neighborhood," I say.

"…the bodies of José Ignacio, Santiago Peréz, Joaquín Zamora…"

"That's Papá's name!" I cry.

"…and Evelin Morena were found piled…"

"The bodies, Mamá? What are they saying?"

A soft wail escapes from Mamá's mouth, *Ay mi Joaquín, por Díos. ¡No!* and grows steadily into a scream. Mamá grabs me and squeezes me so hard I feel like my ribs are going to crack. She's rocking us both together, back and forth, shaking and sobbing, sobbing and shaking. She won't let me breathe! Nico slides off the seat onto the floor, startles awake, and looks up at me. "Mamá, what's wrong?" he asks.

"Hush, Nico," I tell him. "Everything's all right. We're just going on a little trip. Mamá's sad, that's all."

But something is really, really wrong. Mamá's acting crazy and on the radio they're talking about Papá's body. I feel my stomach tighten like a fist and rise to my throat. "Mamá, why are you crying?" Nico asks. "Don't cry." She doesn't even hear him. Oscar's face is in his hands. The driver is banging the steering wheel with his fist. Nico and I grab onto each other. And I can't keep this thought from running through my head: Papá is dead.

8

TORTILLITA, TORTILLITA, PARA MAMÁ

We're in Mexico now and I'm climbing the steps onto another bus. I'm tried. I'm hungry. I can barely lift my feet. A man carrying a basketful of live chickens bumps me out of his way. A woman tugging a little girl up the stairs knocks me down. I sit on the step and don't move. I don't know where I am or where I'm going and I don't care.

Someone grabs my elbow and pulls me to stand. It's Oscar. "Come on, Mario. Else we won't get a seat." He cups his hands on my shoulders and steers me down the aisle to where Mamá and Nico sit huddled against a window. "You sit for the first part," Oscar tells me. "Then we'll trade off." He hands me a tortilla filled with beans. I take one bite, then another. There's a hole in my stomach that not even a dozen tortillas could fill.

How many days have we been traveling? Two or three? All the hours and days of waiting for people and rides and buses are getting scrambled up with each other. Sometimes I don't know if this is real or if I'm in a dream. Mamá keeps mumbling to herself like a prayer, *en el norte*, we can rest. *En el norte*, we'll be safe. *En el norte*, things will get better. Up north, up north, up north. I don't even listen anymore.

In the seat in front of me, a young couple plays a clapping game with their little girl. *Tortillita, tortillita, para Mamá.* Blanca used to play that game with Nico. *Tortillita, tortillita, para Papá.* Where was Blanca now? Did the soldiers come for her, too? *Tortillita, tortillita, para María.* What did the soldiers do with Papá? Did they really shoot him? Is Papá really dead? *Tortillita, tortillita para mi tía.* The bus bumps along treeless, rocky hills. Where are we? Where is the green of my country?

Oscar taps me on the shoulder. It's my turn to stand. I slide off the seat and grip the edge to keep my balance. If Oscar were Papá, I could squeeze in next to him or sit on his lap. But Oscar isn't Papá. Papá doesn't exist anymore, right? Papá won't talk to me. He won't laugh with me. He won't walk on this earth ever again.

My body rocks back in forth against the other people who stand in the aisle. *Tortillita, tortillita*, the little girl claps. Papá won't ride a bus or eat tortillas or ever hug me again. I gaze out the windows. They're cloudy with dirt from the road. More rocky hills and foreign countryside pass by. How am I ever going to live in a world without Papá?

Finally, we get to the United States. We're sitting in dry scrub grasses along the side of a road in a state called Texas, waiting for another ride from another stranger. Oscar's dozing on the ground, using his bag as a pillow. Mamá has spread out her shawl for Nico. "When's the truck coming, Mamá?" I ask.

"Maybe soon," Mamá says.

"And then we'll be safe?" I ask.

"*Ay*, Mario," Mamá says, sighing. "Almost safe." She bends over and rubs Nico's back. I know what that feels like. The back and forth, the warmth from Mamá's hand, the feeling that everything will be all right. I wish I could curl up and lie down next to Nico. I wish Mamá would stroke my back, too. But I'm supposed to be the man in the family now. Isn't that what Oscar told me? I shouldn't want back rubs any more.

I watch as Nico's eyes gently close. His dark lashes rest on his cheeks in half moons. Mamá gazes into the distance. "How much longer?" I ask.

"Don't keep asking me, *mijo*." Mamá's voice is tired and impatient. She pulls her long black hair, dirty, dull, and tangled now, away from her face. She works it into a braid with her fingers and ties it with a band. Back home, she'd sit on the edge of her bed and use a brush. She'd fix up her hair with silver combs and barrettes. And she'd talk to me, ask questions. Did I eat a good breakfast? Did I have my homework?

Now, Mamá barely talks at all.

I lie down on the shawl next to Nico. A buzzard circles overhead as the pale sun drains all blue from the sky. Cicadas buzz and hum in the brush. "Nico," I whisper in his ear. "Nico, are you awake?"

"Leave Nico alone," Mamá says. "Let him sleep."

"I wasn't going to wake him," I mumble and move away.

I find a flat rock and scrape a road in the dirt. I mold a pile of the dry earth for a hill. I get pebbles to mark an intersection, and carve a road in another direction. It's no good. It doesn't look right at all. I need water to bank up the curve. This road isn't half as good as the ones I used to make with Papá at Abuelo's farm. I flop down on the ground. The sun is hot on my back. I watch a shiny black beetle crawl onto my road and wonder, where is Papá now? Is he watching me build this stupid road from Heaven?

I roll over and stare up into the sky. Okay, Papá. I'm waiting for a sign. A cloud covering the sun or a bird soaring high. Anything. But no sign comes. Papá isn't watching over me. Papá is gone.

I sweep away the pebbles from the intersection. With the flat digging stone, I crush the beetle. Yellow oozes from the insect, but I don't care. I'll forget about Papá. The beetle legs go still. Here, somewhere in the United States, I'm going to have a whole new life, Mamá said. I bury the dead beetle in a hole and cover him with a rock. I smooth out the dirt on my road. A whole new life without Papá.

I must've fallen asleep because the next thing I know, Mamá is shaking me. "Wake up Mario," she says. An old farm truck rumbles up the road and stops.

A man and a woman get out of the truck. They rush to our side. The woman's voice is soft. "Hurry," she says. "There's food and water in the back."

The man helps Nico and Mamá into the truck. He gives Mamá some pillows.

"Mario," Mamá calls out from the truck's bed. "Give me your hand," she says.

I reach up, but then I stop. I shouldn't need Mamá's hand anymore. I hoist my own self into the truck. Oscar follows and crouches down next to me and hands me a bottle of water. As the truck drives away, its tires stir up the dust on the road. Swirling clouds erase our footprints. It's as if we were never there, as if we didn't even exist.

It's dark when the truck brings us to a church. Two gringa women and a priest greet us and take us down some stairs to the basement. "Come this way. That's it. Careful of the stairs. Does anyone need the restroom? It's right across the hall." Mamá leads Nico into the Ladies' room. I hesitate, then follow Oscar into the Men's. I look into the mirror and I don't recognize myself. My shirt is torn and I'm scratched up and covered with dirt. My hair is sticking up all over the place. Oscar stands beside me. His beard is thick and his once lively eyes look hollow. "We're a pretty sorry looking pair, aren't we?" He tosses me a washcloth. It feels good to scrub the dirt from my face, hands, arms, legs.

Cooking smells that I don't recognize come from a kitchen. The women bring steaming bowls of soup to the table. Chile con carne, they call the soup. We eat without speaking, dipping spongy white bread into the thick soup. When our bowls are empty, the women fill them again. Later, they show us the way to a room with cots, blankets, and pillows. My eyes close even before I lie down.

9

PAPÁ'S NOTEBOOK

In the morning, a young priest comes to talk to us. He doesn't look like a priest – he's wearing blue jeans and a regular shirt over the neckband collar. He welcomes us and we pray together for the people of our country and all peoples of the world. Then he tells us that we'll be here for a few days while we get our papers in order. Soon we'll travel a city in northern Texas where people from another church will help us begin our new lives.

"What about Papá?" Nico asks. His little voice is like a knife slicing through the room where everyone is listening quietly. Mamá startles and doesn't answer. "We've told you before, Nico," Oscar says. "Remember? Your papá…" I interrupt him before he can say, 'your papá is dead,' or 'soldiers killed your papá.' "Papá can't come with us," I say. I take Nico's hand. When the priest came this morning he brought in three cardboard boxes and set them on the floor. "Come on, Nico, let's look in the boxes," I say. If Oscar says any more about Papá, Mamá will start crying all over again.

I read the English words on the boxes to Nico, "Men, women, children." Inside is clothing for us. The priest comes over and lays his hand on my back. Then he starts digging through the box of children's clothes. "These look just about right for you," he says to me. He hands me a stack of t-shirts and pants.

Back home, Mamá used to give our old clothes away. Now we're the ones taking other people's clothing. I remember how proud I felt to bundle up our old clothes and help Mamá deliver them to the church back home. I hold up a t-shirt with a turtle painted on it. I wonder about the gringo boy who used to wear it. What would he say about me wearing his old shirt?

Later, Mamá and the priest go over some papers. Temporary papers, the priest called them. Quiet sounds come from a television in the corner where Oscar's watching a news program. One of the women from last night came back and is making sandwiches for us. Nico's playing with some plastic blocks she gave him, making a house for Rana. I'm sharpening my colored pencils getting ready to draw.

"What color is this?" I ask Nico in English as I hold up each pencil.

"Red," he says. Then, "Blue. Green." He gets all the colors right except for orange. He has trouble saying the word. "Narange," he says.

"Orange," I say.

"Norange, " he says, giggling.

"Orange!" I say.

"Orangi," he says and starts laughing. Nico makes up more funny color words, and we both fall into hysterics. It's the first time we've laughed since El Salvador and it feels like we never want to stop.

Oscar comes over to see what's so funny. Nico picks up a pencil. "This is a norange pencil," he says and giggles.

Oscar twiddles a pencil through his fingers and looks at me. "Going to be a writer someday like your father?" His question takes our laughter right out of the air. The color game is over.

"These pencils are for drawing," I say.

"Even an artist can use colored pencils to write a few words, *eh, compa?*" Oscar says. I know Oscar's just trying to be clever, but I wish he would stop talking about pencils and Papá and leave me alone. "When I get settled," Oscar says, "I'm going to write about what happened to your father. Joaquín had connections with the *New York Times.* You were there, weren't you?

"There?" I ask.

"You were a witness. You saw the soldiers take him."

I shrug and sharpen another pencil.

Oscar won't shut up. "People here should know. They only way they're going to find out what's really going on is from people like us. Maybe then they'll tell their government to stop sending money and weapons."

I give Nico a yellow pencil "Hey, Nico, what color is this? Hello?" I ask. "Hello, yellow. Get it, Nico?" Laugh, Nico. Come on. Make another joke. I don't want to talk to Oscar. I don't want to talk about what happened to Papá. Doesn't Oscar get that I'm not thinking about that anymore?

"Sorry, Mario," Oscar says, tousling my hair. "I didn't mean to upset you."

"I'm not upset," I say.

That night, after Nico is asleep, Mamá sits on my cot. "I have something for you. From Papá."

"Papá?" I ask.

"I brought it from home. Papá wanted you to have this. I was waiting until we reached sanctuary." She hands me a package. It feels like a book. I untie the string and pull back the paper. Inside is a notebook with a hard black cover. Drawing paper? Maybe Papá was saving it for my birthday. I open the cover. The first page is filled with writing.

My heart stops. I'm all shaky inside. It's Papá's handwriting. The same writing as in the little stories Papá used to write to go with my pictures. The same handwriting as in the framed poem that used to hang on a wall in our house. I used to pass it in the hall every day. It was a love poem Papá wrote to Mamá when they first met.

Seeing Papá's handwriting, the loopy 'y's, the slanted cross on the 't's, it's like Papá is still alive. I can see

Papá bent over his desk. Reading and writing late into the night. Turning his head, his face brightening when he sees me. Opening his arms for a kiss good night. I take a deep breath and read.

> *Dear Mario,*
>   *If you are reading this letter, it means the soldiers have taken me, and you and Mamá and Nico have fled the country.*
>   *You must be brave and strong, Mario.*

What is this? Why did Papá write to me? I slam the notebook shut. "Papá knew?" I cry to Mamá. "He knew the soldiers might come? He knew we might have to leave?"

"*Ay*, Mario," Mamá says. "I shouldn't have…"

"Papá knew he might get killed and he kept writing anyway?" Papá's letter covers a full page, but there's no way I'm going to read one more word.

"I'm so sorry," Mamá says. "I thought having something from Papá would make you feel better." Tears are gathering in her eyes.

"Don't worry, Mamá. I'm fine," I say. I open the notebook and flip through the pages like I'm interested. I make my eyes blur over Papá's words.

My stomach cramps up. I fold the notebook back to a blank page in the middle. I take a pencil and outline a mountain. My head begins to throb around my eyes. I hate this feeling. If I don't catch it in time, I'll start crying. How about a donkey? My picture needs a donkey. First I draw the head, then I add the body and legs. I cover the donkey with a blanket. I put a curving road under the animal and a palm tree at the edge of the page.

Then my fingers take over. They draw a rifle, leaning against the tree. They add a line of smoke, smoldering from the tip of the gun. I rip out the picture, crumple it up, and throw it in the trash.

10

THE FINE SON

Days later, the priest tells us that places have been found for us to live in a city up north. Oscar can stay with a family and continue classes at the university. Across town, there's a place for Mamá, Nico, and me. A member of the church there owns apartments. We can stay in one for free, the priest says, for as long as it takes, until Mamá finds work and is able to pay rent.

So we pack up our things and fill a plastic bag with clothing from the boxes. Another 'friend of the church' picks us up in a van. Outside, I'm seeing the church for the first time. The building looks like a triangle that grows right from the ground. I study its lines. I've never seen anything like it. We've been kept in the basement for days. It's not legal for us to be in this country. Until we get our papers, someone from immigration could arrest us and send us back to El

Salvador. I heard Oscar tell the priest that if we got sent back, we'd be put in jail, or, worse, killed.

I look at the triangle church and I don't want to leave. It's not fun living in a church basement, but I got used to it. Now I have no idea where we're going. I take out the notebook, open to my drawing section, and draw a picture of the church to remember it.

Mamá, Nico, and Oscar get in the van. Soon we're on the highway heading north.

Hundreds of cars zoom past on the wide highway. I've never seen so many different kinds of cars at once. Big cars, small cars, trucks, vans – in reds, blues, silvers, all kinds of colors – whiz by. Traveling on this busy highway is nothing like going to Abuelo's village back home. There, as soon as you get outside the city, the paved road turns to dirt. All you see on the roads there are a few delivery trucks and military jeeps, and pairs of oxen pulling carts full of sugar cane, coffee, and corn.

I lean my head against the window and watch the cars race by. I close my eyes. I wish we were going to Abuelo's and not some strange city in Texas. I wish we could spend the day at his farm, chasing after the chickens, climbing trees, listening to his cook sing in the kitchen. I remember the last time we visited Abuelo's farm for Sunday dinner. Was it only two weeks ago? Two of Abuelo's private guards met us at the gates. They patrolled the property while we ate dinner.

That day, Papá laughed too loudly at Abuelo's jokes and Mamá barely touched her food. We left right after dinner instead of walking down to the pond to see the ducks. And when it came time to say good-bye, Abuelo forgot to slip the handfuls of coins in Nico's and my pockets as he usually did.

As we left the *finca* that day, I heard Abuelo say to Papá. "It's dangerous for you to be here. Don't come back until I tell you." Abuelo's eyes had narrowed then when he'd looked at Papá. He'd kissed me and tickled Nico as if nothing was changed. But now I wonder, had Abuelo been angry with Papá for what he wrote in the newspaper? Was he giving Papá a warning?

A car without a muffler roars past our van. Loud music blares from its opened windows. My eyes pop open. This is no bus ride to visit Abuelo. Papá isn't sitting with us, making up funny names for the *garrobo* lizards that scampered off the side of the road. Mamá isn't singing songs to Nico. This is a van, in the United States, traveling on a big highway. It isn't bringing us to an afternoon of fun at Abuelo's house. We're going to some strange new place we're supposed to call home. A shiver crawls across my back. Will anything in my life ever feel right?

It's late afternoon when the van pulls into a driveway next to a wooden house. Brown paint is peeling off worn shingles. A woman sits on the porch in a white plastic chair, her hands folded around a book in her lap. A nest of white hair is piled on top of her head. When the van stops, she stands up and waves. She walks down the steps to greet us. The driver gets out and sets our things on a line of grass that divides the driveway from the house next door.

This tall church lady glances at her papers. "You must be Mrs. Zamora," she says, peering down at Mamá over half glasses.

"Yes. I am María Elena," Mamá says in her careful English. I still can't get used to Mamá speaking English or the way she looks. Mamá is wearing blue jeans and a red sweatshirt from the boxes. At home, Mamá used to dress in ironed blouses and neat slacks. She chose jewelry from the painted box on her bureau and never left the house without lipstick.

"And glad to meet you, Mario. I'm Mrs. Harrison." She shakes my hand. "You must be exhausted from your trip. And hungry. Don't worry, we've stocked the apartment with lots of food. Am I talking too fast? It says here you speak English, is that right?"

"I speak a little," says Mamá. "But Mario knows from going to the English school in El Salvador." Just then, Nico pulls away from Mamá and starts running down the sidewalk. In the street, cars rush by.

"Nico!" I yell. A truck screeches to a stop. The driver honks his horn. More cars come speeding down the two-lane road. "Look out!" I grab Nico and make him stop.

Nico pulls away. "Chase me! Chase me!" he says.

"Stop it, Nico! This isn't a game," I say.

"What a fine son you have, Mrs. Zamora. To watch out for his little brother like that," Mrs. Harrison says.

"Look at our new house!" I tell Nico. "This is where we're going to live now." I point to the clapboard house with the shades pulled down on all the windows. "And this will be our new neighborhood." At the corner, a bus stops for a man with a folded-up shopping cart. A group of teenagers walk down the sidewalk listening to loud music on a boom-box. Across the street a mother yells. "Time for supper!" On the porch a black dog wags his tail as kids come up the stairs. "Look, Nico! See there? See the dog?"

I'm talking in an excited voice to keep Nico happy, but everything here looks and feels so different. The houses, the wide streets with big cars, tall Mrs. Harrison with her papers and bushy white hair. Even the air doesn't smell right.

We don't belong here. We belong back in El Salvador, going to our own school, playing with friends, with Papá waiting for us with some new surprise from the university store. If only we could go back. I wouldn't complain any more about riding with Señor Perez. I wouldn't talk to strangers. Everything would be better at home. Soldiers and curfews and all.

11

CHICKEN NOODLE SOUP

Mrs. Harrison leads us upstairs to a second-floor apartment. In places along the stairway, the wallpaper is torn and hanging from the walls. She opens the door to our apartment. It smells like fresh paint and these walls are all a shiny white. "This is the living room," she says. "The couch unfolds into a bed. Mario, you can sleep here." In another room are two beds for Mamá and Nico. Then she shows us the bathroom. She pulls aside a shower curtain with pictures of fish on it. "Watch," she says, turning on the water. "The water's a little tricky and it takes forever for the hot to come on."

We end up in the kitchen. Plastic bags and boxes of clothes and toys cover the kitchen table. Nico reaches for a toy truck and gives Rana a ride in it along the table's top. Mamá tousles Nico's hair. "Everyone is being so good to us in this country," Mamá says to me. She nudges me. "Thank you, Mrs. Harrison," I say.

Next, Mrs. Harrison opens the kitchen cabinets. They are filled with cans of soup, boxes of pasta, breakfast cereals. "All this food has been donated by people from our church," Mrs. Harrison says.

"They're very generous," says Mamá.

"I want to show you how the stove works," Mrs. Harrison says. "What kind of soup do you want for your first supper in your new home, Mario? Chicken noodle, chicken and rice, tomato…?"

"Chicken noodle," I say.

Mrs. Harrison opens the soup, pours it into a pan, adds water, and lights the stove. While the soup heats up, she points out the window. "Look, Mario. There's your school right down the street."

I have to crane my head to see out the window. At the end of the street is a red brick building with a big playground surrounded by grass and trees. On one side of the school is a painted mural with animals, trees, flowers, people. I squint to read the sign. *Welcome to Butler School*, it says. A giant pencil hangs over the entrance.

Later, Mamá, Nico and I sit around the kitchen table, eating our first meal in the new apartment: chicken noodle soup with white crackers from a box. I don't like the taste of the soup. It's too salty and the noodles are slimy. "Mamá, can't we make some rice, too?" I ask. "Or…," I was going to say, can we try another can of soup, but Mamá's not listening. She's lost in her own world, staring at the empty chair across from her, the chair where Papá should be.

Mamá and Nico fall asleep quickly as I lie on the couch in a strange room, staring at the ceiling. I hear cars whoosh by in the street. A streetlight shines in a pale wedge of light. A siren wails in the distance. The room fills with loneliness. I take out the notebook from Papá. Maybe Mamá was right. Maybe having something from Papá would make me feel better. I flip through the pages and turn to Papá's letter. I read the beginning again.

> *Dear Mario,*
> *If you are reading this letter, it means the soldiers have taken me, and you and Mamá and Nico have fled the country.*
> *You must be brave and strong, Mario.*

I hold my breath and keep reading.

> *Be a good son to Mamá. Help her with Nico so he'll grow up to be a smart boy just like you. Teach Nico to be honest and kind, and to do good for others as I have tried to teach you.*

The good son. The smart boy. Honest and kind. I slam the notebook shut. When did Papá write this letter anyway? Did he know what was going to happen? Then why did he get our family in trouble? My eyes begin to smart. I press them with the heels of my hands. I wish I could go back home and wrap myself in my favorite blanket, in my own bed, with the sounds of Papá's typewriter outside my door.

Suddenly, Papá's voice comes into his head. Not his kind and playful voice, not even his strict voice, but a new voice, a pleading voice. *Don't let me down, mijo. Nico needs you. Mamá needs you. Por favor, don't let me down.*

I get up and stand at the window. At night, spotlights shine on the entrance to the Butler School. Papá doesn't need to worry. I'll be a good boy. I'll watch after Mamá and Nico. And I'll work hard at school, just like he'd want me to.

I'll be my better self.

12

BUTLER SCHOOL

Mrs. Harrison meets us at the apartment to take Nico and me for our first day at Butler School. She has found a job for Mamá, cleaning houses for some of the people who go to her church. Nico will go into the kindergarten and an after-school program. I'll be in the fifth grade. She explains all this to us as we walk towards the school.

Up ahead, on the playground, kids are running around and playing. Some are shooting baskets. Others chase each other around a jungle gym. One girl dangles her feet from the top rung. On the front steps to the school, a small group is standing around a boy who's holding up a poster. Everyone's talking and laughing. I hang back while the others cross the street.

"It'll be all right, Mario," Mrs. Harrison says. "Your teacher's expecting you. He knows your situation. Your mother said you had lots of friends at home. I'm sure you'll make friends here, too."

We pass the kids on the playground and walk into the school. The school's hallway walls are covered with kids' pictures and compositions. A teacher leads a silent line of little kids down the hall, their colorful lunch boxes bouncing against their legs.

"This is Miss Radville, your teacher," Mrs. Harrison says, taking Nico's hand. Miss Radville's face brightens with a smile as she shakes Nico's hand. She puts a hand on his shoulder. They stand together, holding the classroom door as the kindergarteners file in. Then she gently guides Nico in ahead of her. Over her shoulder she nods and smiles at Mamá. Nico goes in with the other children. He doesn't even look back. Nico must be much braver than I am.

Next, Mrs. Harrison leads us up a set of stairs. "And here's your room," she tells me as she taps on the door to room 216. She pushes the door open. "Here's the boy I was telling you about, Mr. Sandowski," she says.

"Mrs. Harrison, hello." Mr. Sandowski's wearing a blue shirt with a necktie that looks like children have drawn pictures all over it. He has a round smiling face, wire-rimmed glasses, and not much brown hair.

I look around the classroom. Plastic cups sit on the windowsill with green seedlings poking out. The desks are set up in clusters of four or five, not like my old school, where we sat at long tables, arranged in rows. This classroom is full of stuff: shelves packed with books, bright posters on the walls, shoeboxes filled with cut-out people and scenes. In the back of the room is an aquarium with real fish swimming around. Planet mobiles sway back and forth with the breeze that comes through the open windows. I've never even imagined a classroom like this.

"Mario, is it?" Mr. Sandowski asks, extending his hand. I nod.

"I'm Mr. Sandowski, Mario. I teach everything to the fifth graders except art and gym. The art teacher won't let me near her supplies, and I start tripping over my feet if I get anywhere near a gymnasium. What about you, Mario? What do you like to do?"

I shrug. He's talking so fast and I can't make my mouth speak.

"Reading? Math? Basketball? Music?" Mr. Sandowski continues.

"I like to draw," I say.

"Ah, drawing," Mr. Sandowski says. "Good for you. We can always use another artist in our class. We've just started working on our class play. Maybe you could help with the scenery?"

A play? On a stage with sets? We never put on plays back home. Soft music comes out of a cassette player on his desk. Mr. Sandowski seems nice. Maybe this school won't be so bad after all.

"There's a desk all set up for you," Mr. Sandowski says. "Have a seat. Take a look at the books inside. The bell's going to ring any minute." Kids are gathered around the classroom door, peering in.

I sit at the desk as Mr. Sandowski and Mrs. Harrison talk at the front of the room. I lift the lid. Inside are books, notebooks, pencils and pens, a ruler, and a calculator. I switch it on, add up some numbers, then subtract them again. I put a pencil in the compass and draw a pattern of circles on a piece of paper.

Mamá comes over and kisses me good-bye like I'm a little boy. I glance at the doorway. Are the kids watching this? Then Mrs. Harrison comes over and pats me on the shoulder. She gives me money for lunch. I want to crawl under the desk.

Brrrrriiiing! rings the school bell. Thankfully, Mamá and Mrs. Harrison leave the classroom. The kids burst in, not in single file as we had to back home, but in groups of talking children. Kids put papers in a basket on Mr. Sandowski's desk, sharpen their pencils, water their plants. One kid sprinkles food for the fish. A boy writes the day and date in chalk on the board. Another boy shows Mr. Sandowski a folder with papers in it. "Excellent job, William," Mr. Sandowski says to the boy. I notice a small cardboard box on Mr. Sandowski's desk. Suggestion Box, it says. Soon, a girl with a head full of beaded braids sits down next to me.

"Hi! You're Mario, right?" she asks.

I nod.

"Mr. Sandowski told us you were coming today. You're from El Salvador, right?"

I nod again.

"You speak English, don't you?" she asks. The beads in her hair click as she unzips and unloads her backpack.

"Yes, we spoke English in my old school."

"I'm LaShaunda." I notice she arranges her books, pencils, and pens very carefully on her desk. The William boy comes over and hands her a notebook. "You must have mine," he says. "This is yours." They exchange notebooks and LaShaunda introduces him. He's her twin brother.

Then a tall, thin boy with hair the color of sand bumps against LaShaunda's desk and makes her pencils roll off. "Cut it out, Randall," LaShaunda says. She puts the pencils back right where they were.

"Sorry, little Miss Perfect," Randall says. He drops his books on the desk next to mine and sits down. Leaning back, he flops an arm over the back of the chair. "Hey, LaShaunda," he says. "Who's your new boyfriend?"

"Shut up," says LaShaunda. "Mario, that's Randall. Ignore him."

Just then Mr. Sandowski starts clapping in a pattern. Clap- clap-clap-clap-clap, clap-clap! I look around the classroom. One by one, the kids start clapping with him.

"What are you doing?" I ask LaShaunda.

She laughs. "Oh, that's how he gets us to pay attention."

The morning slips by. Mr. Sandowski reads us a poem by Robert Frost. I've seen the poem before!

It was in our English book back home. Then Mr. Sandowski asks me and William to pass around books to all the students. *Hi, Mario. Thanks, Mario,* the kids say to me as I put the books on their desks. And when Mr. Sandowski puts a math problem on the board, I don't raise my hand, but I know the answer.

"Who's hungry?" Mr. Sandowski asks. Already it's lunchtime. Some kids get lunch boxes from the closet, others line up at the door. "Do you have a token?" LaShaunda asks me.

"Token?"

"You have to get one from Mr. Sandowski for lunch," she says. "Do you have money?"

"Yes," I say.

"Come with me." LaShaunda leads me to Mr. Sandowski's desk.

"Whatever would Mario do without you?" Randall says, snickering.

LaShaunda rolls her eyes and says nothing.

LaShaunda and I are the last to line up, and the line is moving slowly into the cafeteria. As we wait in the hall, I look to the front of the line. Randall is talking to a group of the little kids. He looks like a giant next to them. Nico is leaving the cafeteria with another little boy. They stop at the bubbler, stand on tiptoes, and take a drink. Nico sees me, points me out to his friend, and waves. I wave back. In our other school, Nico and I were in different buildings. We never saw each other. I like seeing Nico here. It makes me feel like this is my school, too.

I glance at Randall. One of the little kids is handing him a small glass snow globe. Randall holds the globe up and turns it in his hand. White sparkles swirl around inside. Then Randall takes the globe and puts it in his backpack. The little kid's face gets all scrunched up as Randall walks away.

When the school day is over and we're packing up to leave, I notice Randall take the snow globe from his backpack and shake it. He catches me staring at him. "What are you looking at, Punk-Face?" he asks.

I don't know what Punk-Face means, but I can tell it's not nice. "Nothing," I say and gather books from my desk. There is one thing I don't like about this school – and that's Randall.

13

OPEN WINDOWS

At the end of the day, I leave the school and head for the apartment. Nico stays in a program for little kids after school, but I am supposed to go home and wait for Mamá. Kids run off in different directions. Some board yellow school busses that line up on the street. Others get into waiting cars. I see LaShaunda unlock her bike from the bike rack and take off down the street. "Bye, Mario. See you tomorrow," she says and waves to me.

I wait at the corner for the light to change. A mother stands with a little kid – he looks like a first grader – looking through his papers. "What's this note from your teacher, Jeffrey?" she asks. "She had to lend you lunch money? I sent you to school with lunch money!"

"It got lost," the boy says.

"That's the second time this week. I have a mind to…" she says. The light changes and she pulls him across the street. I go the other way so I don't hear the rest of what she says.

I run up the stairs to my apartment and lock and bolt the door behind me. I go to the phone in the kitchen and dial the number on a piece of paper taped to the phone. It's Mrs. Harrison's number. I call her to tell her I'm home safely.

"Very good, Mario," she says. She asks me about my day at the school, then says, "Remember, stay in the apartment, just as we planned. Your mom will be home soon with Nico."

I hang up the phone and look around the apartment. It's so quiet and empty. What if someone came in during the day and is hiding, waiting in a closet to attack me or kidnap me? Mario, don't be such a baby, I tell myself. Still, I look in Mamá's room, under the bed. I peek behind the shower curtain. I move the couch away from the wall. No one is here. I turn on the radio. All I hear is static. I move around the dial until I hear music from a Spanish radio station.

I get crackers from the cabinet and pour myself a glass of milk. I'm sitting at the table, by myself, chewing on crackers, and listening to Spanish music. I'm wishing my best friend, Beto, from home were here with me. "Hey, Beto," I whisper. "How's it going?" In my mind, I'm telling him about the new school. "We've got fish in our classroom," I think/say. "Isn't that cool? "But there's this kid, Randall…"

"On sale now! At MidTown Motor City!" The radio shouts out a commercial in English. The Spanish music is gone. What stupid game am I playing? That Beto is sitting across from me, talking about school? I put the crackers back in the box and click off the radio. Beto's far away, back home El Salvador. Probably kicking around a soccer ball with friends in the park. Or, have soldiers come for his father, too? No. Why would they? Beto's father sold plumbing supplies. What would soldiers care about that?

I leave the kitchen and go to stare out the front windows. Thick buds are bulging from the magnolia trees. Mrs. Harrison said that in a few weeks the flowers would make a canopy over the street. I open a window for air, listen to the birds.

Then I go sit on the couch. Next to me is a table covered with books Mrs. Harrison has brought for Nico and me. I flip through the books. In the pile is Papá's notebook. With Papá's letter inside. It's Papá's fault that I'm stuck in this apartment, away from my friends and everything I used to know. Papá and the newspaper and his stupid writing. Why couldn't Papá sell plumbing supplies like Beto's father? Why did he have to write articles in the paper for all the world to see? He could have listened to Abuelo. Or Mamá. He could've listened to Mamá and left the city. Papá knew what could happen. He didn't stop to think about his family. He didn't care that we'd be sent away.

My head is pounding. I cradle it in my arms. Stop thinking, Mario. Stop thinking! I have to get rid of these horrible thoughts about Papá now running through my head. I reach for the notebook. Please. Papá. Let there be something in your letter to make me stop. An explanation. Something. I open the book.

Papá's letter continues:

> *My son, I know how you must be suffering. Please don't hold the pain in your heart. Use this notebook to write to me, Mario. When you write, pretend I'm here to read what you say. Writing helps take away the sorrow.*

I stop. What is Papá saying to me now? That I should write to him? What was Papá thinking? Did Papá think dead people could read from Heaven? How can you write to a person who's dead? Besides, what good would it do? Papá was the writer in the family, not me. So why is he asking me?

With each thought, the knots in my stomach twist tighter. I open the notebook to my drawing pages and go back to the kitchen. A picture. I will draw a picture of the aquarium. I will draw every single fish and stone. I'll make up new fishes. I've filled half a page with crazy fish when I hear voices outside the front windows.

Down below, on the sidewalk across the street, are two kids from school, LaShaunda and William.

They're waiting for the light to change so they can cross. LaShaunda bounces a soccer ball on her knee. William grabs it in the air and balances it on top of his head, moving around like his body is made of elastic. LaShaunda starts laughing and scoops the ball out of the air from William.

Get it, William, I think. Grab it back! The light changes and they cross the street until they're right under my windows. I can hear their voices.

"Man, I am so thirsty," says William.

"We can get drinks at JP's," says LaShaunda, tossing the ball.

"Hey!" I yell out the window. "Hey, LaShaunda! William! Up here!" But the two kids don't hear me. They go around the corner and disappear.

14

MAP READING

Tonight Mrs. Harrison is driving us to her church for a meeting. Nico and I are in the back seat playing a guessing game about things we see out the window. You only get to ask three questions before you have to guess. "You go first," I say. "Find something."

Nico looks out the window. "Okay, I'm ready," he says.

"What shape is it?" I ask.

"Round," Nico says.

"What color is it?" I ask.

"Green."

"Is it alive? I ask.

"No," Nico answers.

"That's obvious. It's the green traffic light!" I say.

"No, it's an eyeball," says Nico.

"An eyeball? You can't see someone's eyeball from here. Besides eyeballs are alive."

Nico doesn't care. "I win! You're turn," he says.

Up front, Mrs. Harrison is talking to Mamá. "There's no need to be nervous," she says. "Just talk naturally. The people at the meeting are friends. They want to hear first-hand about what's going on in El Salvador so they can figure out ways to help. They're going to ask you about your husband, María Elena, and what happened."

My ears prick up. I lean forward. "Why do *you* have to talk to them, Mamá?" I ask. "Why do they have to know about Papá?"

Mamá turns around and reaches to place a hand on my cheek, but she doesn't answer.

"It's called giving testimony, Mario," Mrs. Harrison says. "When people hear your story, it makes what's happening in your country more real. Then maybe our country can help put an end to this war."

I think of Oscar wanting to write for that newspaper in New York.

"And we can go home?" Nico asks.

"Ay, *mijo.* I wish it were that simple," says Mamá.

Don't say what you're thinking, a voice inside me warns. Just sit still and find something out the window for Nico to guess. But words begin to spill out of my mouth anyway. "We can't go back, can we, Mamá? Not ever. And it's because of Papá, isn't it?" My heart pounds like a hammer in my chest. "Papá didn't have to write those stupid articles, you know."

"Mario, have respect," Mamá says.

"It's your turn, Mario," Nico says.

I should shut up. I should play with Nico. But I can't stop myself. "Papá should've thought of us," I say. "He only cared about what he wanted to do. He could've …"

"Find something for me to guess," Nico orders.

"Mario," Mrs. Harrison says. "I know it's hard for you to understand, but your father was a courageous man. He knew what was at stake for your country."

"What about his family?" I ask.

Mrs. Harrison continues. "People who stay silent in the face of injustice and brutality help keep it going."

Yeah, but they're still alive, I think.

Mamá turns around to look at me. "Mrs. Harrison knows some people. They're working now to get Nicolás out of the country."

"Tío Nicolás?" I ask.

"That's right, Mario," says Mrs. Harrison. "If we can get him out, there are people here who are very interested in what he has to say. Your uncle is willing to share important information about the government."

My head is swimming with all Mrs. Harrison's fancy words – injustice, brutality, important information. The thought of seeing Tío Nicolás again is like a raft in a stormy sea of words.

The meeting hall smells like floor wax and fresh coffee. Adults are standing around a table, pouring cups of coffee, and talking. Cookies are piled high in pyramids on trays. Chocolate, plain, some with sprinkles, some with jelly in the middle. I've never seen so many kinds of cookies. Mamá has told me to keep an eye on Nico during the meeting. I hold his hand as we walk around the room.

Nico tugs at my arm, pulling me toward the table.

"No cookies," I say.

Mrs. Harrison calls us over to the folding chairs that are set up in rows. "You and Nico sit here, Mario," she says. "Right up front." Mamá's sitting at a long table facing the audience with Oscar and two other people I don't know from El Salvador. On the wall behind the table is a map of El Salvador.

I stare at the map's familiar shape. It's like seeing a picture of an old friend you haven't seen in a long time. My eyes zero in on the capital, San Salvador. I stare hard at the black dot. I wish that black dot would get bigger and bigger and suck me and Mamá and Nico right back to El Salvador.

"We're ready to begin," Mrs. Harrison says. "I'd like to introduce María Elena Zamora, a woman of true courage. And Mario," she turns to me. "Could you please stand, too?"

I stand up.

"Go ahead, turn around so the people can see you," Mrs. Harrison says. "And this is Mario, the brave son, who, overnight, had to pack away his childhood and enter an adult world of violence, secrecy, and despair."

Everyone is clapping and staring at me. The man next to me cups a hand on my shoulder and holds it there. As if he is, all of a sudden, my best friend.

"And Mario's little brother, Nico," Mrs. Harrison says, looking around the room. "Nico, where are you?"

Nico's over by the cookie table. He's reaching up, pulling on the edge of a tray. "Nico!" I yell. The whole pyramid topples over. Cookies scatter everywhere: on the table, under the table, and over the floor. Some people start chuckling. A woman gets up and picks up the fallen cookies.

"Mario!" Mamá's voice cuts through the commotion. "*¡Quita al Nico de allí!*" Get Nico away from there!

I grab Nico's arm. "Don't worry, Maria Elena," Mrs. Harrison tells Mamá. "Let the boys help themselves to cookies." We each take a handful. Then Mrs. Harrison takes Nico and me down the hall from where the people are speaking into a room full of toys. Nico finds a plastic school bus and little plastic people that go in it. "Help me, Mario," he says, handing me a fistful of the figures.

As I help Nico fill the bus, I hear Oscar's voice booming down the hall: "I speak for those who cannot speak for themselves," he's saying. "Imagine an entire village of people, fleeing from their homes, running through the night. Innocent men, women, and children, abandoning their village to hide in caves.

"And after fourteen days, when hunger causes the children to cry out, the soldiers find them. One by one, the soldiers pull these innocent people from their hiding places and order them to march. An old woman, too weak from hunger to obey, is killed, her body left in the cave."

For a long moment, there is silence. In my mind, I see them – weak, tired, hungry, huddled together in dark caves. Then people begin asking questions. Where did the incident take place? How many were killed? What happened to the village?

Nico stands up. The toy school bus is full. He pushes the bus so hard that it crashes into the wall. All the little people fall out. Nico cries out in delight. "Let's do it again!" Nico says, running over to the toys. Nico hasn't been paying attention to Oscar's story. He's just a little kid who wants to play. He picks up the bus and brings it to me. Then he runs back and forth to collect all the people. As, one by one, he puts them back in the bus, I think about the people in that village. I know my country is at war, but villagers hiding in caves, starving without food? Old women being shot by soldiers? Is that a part of war, too?

15

HOOPS AND WHEELS

At recess, William and some of the other boys have been teaching me to play basketball. Today, it rained all morning and the kindergarteners didn't get to go out for their morning recess, so they're outside this afternoon with us fifth graders. Between turns practicing shooting baskets, I look over at Nico. He's climbing the jungle gym at the far end of the playground with a group of little kids. He gets to the top, hooks his knees over the bar, hangs upside down, holds onto the bar with one hand, and waves to me with the other. My little brother looks funny like that, hanging upside down. His hair sticks straight down like one of those cartoon characters with his hand in a socket.

"Heads up, Mario!" William yells and tosses me the ball. I dribble it a few times then set myself up to try and land a basket. "That's it. Nice and easy. Remember, make it curve in the air," William says.

I shoot. The ball makes a nice arc just like William's taught me. It's heading toward the basket. Not too high for once, and not off center. Come on, ball, go in. Go in! It bounces off the rim into the next boy's hands.

"You almost got it that time," William says.

Randall, who spends most of his recess just wandering around, passes by and laughs at me. "Nice shot, Punk-Face," he says.

"Let's see you try," I say.

"Why should I? Basketball's stupid," he says and runs off.

Later, William has me practicing foot drills. First, two feet together, jumping side to side over a line. Then one foot at a time. Then the same thing in a circle, clockwise and counterclockwise. He gets me so out of breath, I don't care when the bell rings to go inside. We run to the school door and wait for the other kids to fall in line.

The kindergarteners stay out longer. As I'm waiting, panting my head off, I look to see if Nico's still on the jungle gym. I wave but he doesn't see me this time. Randall's over there, sitting on the little kids' merry-go-round, pushing it with his feet to make it go faster and faster. I see Nico's teacher move toward him and gesture for him to stop and get off. Randall always waits for the very last second to come in from recess.

That afternoon, I'm sitting in the apartment after school, drawing. I had an idea to draw kids playing basketball, one dribbling, one getting ready to shoot, one jumping to catch a ball, but when I sit down to start drawing, who shows up on the page? The villagers in the cave. I draw them sitting against the walls of cave, crowded together. Then I remember the hunger and I don't know what to do about that. Did they bring food with them, or were they in too much of a hurry? I make a wood fire and put on a pot of rice and beans. I give one man a guitar to play, and a flute to another.

When my picture is done, I close the notebook. Mrs. Harrison said she's trying to get us a T.V. I sure wish we had one now. Mamá and Nico won't be home for two-and-a-half hours. There's nothing to do around here except read, draw, or do my homework. Out the window I hear the sounds of the street – buses grumbling past, cars honking, our neighbor calling her dog, "Bernie, here Bernie. Bernie, come here!" I crouch down and lean against the windowsill. I can almost pretend I'm outside. Almost.

"How many seconds before the light changes?" someone asks.

"I say, twenty-five."

"I say, fifty."

"Okay, count! One, two, three …"

It's LaShaunda and William. They're on bicycles, waiting to cross the street. Silently, I count with them. The light changes in forty-seven seconds. William wins. They walk their bikes across the street.

"Hey," I yell. "Up here!"

They look up. "Mario!" LaShaunda calls. "What are you doing? Want to go riding with us?"

"Can't. I have homework," I say.

"That math worksheet? It only takes a second," says William.

"And I don't have a bike," I say.

LaShaunda and William look at each other. "Should I?" William asks.

"Yeah," says LaShaunda.

"I'll be right back," William says.

"Where are you going?"

"We have an old one at home," LaShaunda says.

"But…" I say.

"Don't worry. We live right around the corner," LaShaunda says. "It'll only take a second."

Before I can say anything, William's waving, *see you later*, running across the street and around the corner. I'm not allowed to leave the apartment. And now William's going to bring me a bike?

"Come on down," LaShaunda calls up to me.

I can't go down there. Or, can I? *Don't start thinking what you're thinking, Mario*, I warn myself. Could I leave? Should I leave? Would Mamá find out? I look around the apartment. The empty apartment.

I'm so sick of being stuck here, all alone. LaShaunda's waiting for me. William's getting me a bicycle. If I go down now and tell them I can't go, then William would have to take the bike back. Then what would they think of me? I grab the keys and go downstairs.

William comes back right away with a bike. Sunlight hits the silver on its front fender making it shine. That bike is calling to me: *Come on, Mario. Take a hold of the handlebars, hoist a leg over the bar, and settle in on this nice seat.*

"We're going to the park. Ready?" says William.

Just to the park. It isn't far. No one will ever know. LaShaunda and William are kids from the neighborhood. Their parents let them ride on their own. How could it be dangerous? I glance back at the apartment. I get on the bike and follow LaShaunda and William.

I'm on a bike! A silver bike. The wind's blowing in my face. I'm pumping my legs. I'm gulping deep breaths of fresh air. I'm flying down the street like a bird. Soaring at last. Free. I'm feeling like I used to feel, like a normal boy.

"Follow us!" said LaShaunda.

The wind whistles by my ears. I'll get back way before Mamá comes home. A man is washing his car at the side of the curb, music blaring from the radio inside. A woman comes out of the hardware store carrying a can of paint. I slow down to pass a mother pushing a baby in a stroller. A man pulling a cart of groceries steps to the side and waves. "Nice day for a ride," he says.

"It's a great day for a ride!" I say.

A bus stops at the corner. A boy my age is helping a woman with a cane up the steps. *Be a good son to Mamá.* Out of nowhere, Papá's words come to me. My heart sinks. Does Papá have to follow me everywhere? I should turn back right now, go in the house, lock the door, do my homework. I should wait for Mamá and Nico just like Mamá told me.

But ahead is the park. A group of kids is playing soccer. I know some of them. I haven't touched a soccer ball once since leaving home. And I want to show William there are *some* sports I know how to play. We ride into the park and park the bikes. Someone scores a goal and arms and hands shoot into the air. Everyone cheers. "Hey, want to play?" a boy from school yells. "We could use some more players."

"Sure!" William says, running towards the field. LaShaunda and I follow. "Over here," William yells to a girl dribbling the ball down the sidelines. He gets the ball and boots it over to LaShaunda. "Heads up," LaShaunda says, getting ready to pass it to me. She kicks the ball too hard and it's heading out of bounds. Quickly, I stop the ball with my foot and turn it in the other direction. "Nice save," someone calls. Dribbling down the field, I'm headed to the goal. I'm ready to score.

"Go, Mario!" William yells.

"It's all yours," cries LaShaunda.

My eyes go from the ball, to the goal, to the goalie. I'm setting up the ball and I'm ready to slam it into the goal. Then I look up. Out of nowhere, Scowly-Face's beady eyes and vicious sneer show up in my head. I freeze.

"Kick it, Mario!" William yells.

"Go, Mario, go!" LaShaunda chants.

Another kid glides over from behind and steals the ball away. I kick Scowly-Face out of my head and hurry down the field. I'm running and panting, but I can't catch up. With each step, I pound the soldier's nasty face into the ground. Go away! Pound. Go away! Pound. Go away! Go away! Go away!

The other team scores a goal.

16

On the way home we stop at JP's Variety Store, a block away from the park. LaShaunda has a list of things to buy for her mother. We leave the bikes out front. Bells attached to a leather strap hanging on the door jangle when William opens it.

The man behind the counter is watching a small black-and-white TV. He's wearing a red baseball cap with a frayed visor. The store smells like hot dogs from a steamer on the front counter.

In front of the candy display, a father squats next to a little boy Nico's age. "Only one thing," the father is saying. "Don't touch now. Make up your mind first, then take the candy."

"Come on," says LaShaunda. "Let's find the spaghetti." I go along down an aisle crowded with cereal boxes, jars of tomato sauce, spaghetti, and loaves of bread.

"I'll get the paper towels," William says.

Back at the counter, the little boy has chosen a Sky Bar. The father lifts him so he can give the money to the cashier. Then the father helps the boy tear open the yellow candy wrapper. The boy breaks off a piece and puts it in his mouth.

Last Easter, Papá brought Nico and me a bag of sugar-coated almonds. He laughed at the way we divided the almonds so carefully into small piles on the table. There was one extra. "I'll take care of that one," Papá said, and popped it in his mouth.

LaShaunda pays the man behind the counter. The bells on the door ring again and two teenagers come in.

Now the little boy is breaking off another piece of Sky Bar and giving it to his father. "Why, thank you!" the father says. Father and son chew on their candy.

Papá liked the almond so much, Nico and I made a third pile just for him. When Mamá saw us all happily chewing on our treats, she said she never knew she had three children in the house.

I look around the store. No one's looking. I snatch three Sky Bars and stash them in my pocket.

On the ride back home, I feel a strange excitement. Why shouldn't I take that candy? Where is my father to buy me treats? Nico should have candy, too. I picture breaking the candy in half and handing a piece to Nico. I see Nico's eager face. Nico's reaching for the candy. Stolen candy. Suddenly, flames shoot out from the candy, burning Nico's hand. I stop the bike. What was I thinking? What is happening to me? Sneaking out after school, lying to Mamá, now stealing?

"I forgot something at the store," I say. "I've got to go back."

"Want us to come with you?" William asks.

"No, that's okay. I can find my way. I'll catch up," I say.

I pedal hard. With each pump of the pedal, *brave son, good son, strong son, smart son,* runs through my head. If I can just put the candy back before anyone notices, I promise from now on I'll be all the things Papá ever wanted me to be. I'll obey Mamá, work hard at school, take care of Nico. *Brave son, good son, strong son, smart son:* I'll be someone Papá could be proud of.

I wait until the man behind the counter is looking the other way. Then I sneak in and return the candy bars to the case. Just as I reach to pull open the door to leave, someone calls out my name.

"Hey, Mario," he says. It's Randall. He's come out of the back room.

"Randall?"

"What's going on, Punk-Face? You stealing from my father's store?" he asks.

"No."

"I saw you take that candy. I'd call that stealing, wouldn't you?" Randall says.

"I put it back," I say.

"Stealing is stealing," Randall says, stepping closer to me. He's a full head taller than I am. "See that camera there?" Randall points to a video camera in the corner of the store. "It's always on."

"I put the candy back," I say. "I didn't keep it."

"So? The camera didn't see that. It taped you stealing."

"It was only a candy bar, Randall, and I put it back," I say.

"My father could get you kicked out of the country, you know."

Kicked out of the country? How could I be so stupid – stealing, here, now, before our papers come? I glance at the video camera. I'm an illegal boy, in a country where I don't belong, stealing for all the world to see.

My schoolbooks are spread out on the kitchen table. William was right: the math homework didn't take long. I'm doing the extra problems at the back of the book. I wish there were a whole other book of extra problems. I want to do math problems until my pencils wear out. I hear Mamá at the door and open it for her. Mamá has dark circles under her eyes and her shoulders sag from carrying two sacks of groceries. "Need help putting the food away?" I ask.

Mamá sets down the bag on the kitchen chairs. "Look at all these books. You're working so hard. I could not ask for a better son," Mamá says to me. She holds my face in her hands. "Papá would be so proud."

Papá? Proud? Of me? His son, the liar and thief? Right then, I want to tell Mamá everything. About the candy. About LaShaunda and William. About riding a bike and playing soccer right down the street. And that sometimes I get scared because, in my head, I hear Papá talking to me.

But I unpack the groceries, put the milk in the refrigerator and the fruit in a bowl. I won't tell Mamá any of these things. She has enough sadness and worry already without me adding to her pile.

Nico comes crying into the kitchen. His face is all blotchy. "I can't find him, Mamá. He isn't there. He isn't anywhere."

"Are you sure you looked carefully? Did you look everywhere?" Mamá asks.

"Yes, Mamá. I told you. He's lost forever," Nico yells, stomping his foot and crying.

"What are you talking about?" I ask.

"Nico can't find Rana, you know, that frog he loves so much?" Mamá says.

Nico looks up at me, his eyes glistening with tears, but hopeful. Maybe I know something about his lost toy. I wish I could pull Nico's frog from my pocket or out my ear, but I have no idea where Rana is.

"It was the last thing Papá gave to me," Nico cries. "Now I don't have anything from Papá."

Neither Mamá nor I even try to find words to console him. We understand what Nico has lost.

17

CURRENT EVENTS

It's Friday, current events day. During the week we're supposed to find an article from a newspaper or a magazine, cut it out, and write a paragraph about the event. Then on Fridays, Mr. Sandowski calls on four or five kids to share their current event with the class.

First, a girl named Juliette raises her hand.

"What have you got, Juliette?" Mr. Sandowski asks.

"Something about how they're going to build a new water treatment plant in town," Juliette says.

"Come on up and tell us about it," Mr. Sandowski says.

Juliette goes to the front of the room and talks about the plans for the new plant, the pump station, and filtration system. Then she passes her article and paragraph around the room.

Then a boy named Matt presents his article about a high school student who won a thousand dollars in the science fair.

"A thousand dollars? Wow!" someone says.

"He can't just spend it, you know," Matt says. "He has to use it for college."

Next, a girl named Sarah has her turn in the front of the class. "Some workers at the Car 'n Suds Car Wash were caught this week by special agents. The workers weren't supposed to be living in this country, so the police came and now they're being sent back home to Guatemala. It's called de-por-ta-tion. They've been living here for three years.

"One man has a baby that was born here, and now he has to be sent back to his country. Without his baby. I don't think that's right, Mr. Sandowski, do you?" she asks.

Sarah passes around her paragraph with a photograph from the newspaper mounted on a piece of yellow construction paper. I study the photograph. There's a big Car 'n Suds sign across the top with some cars lined up at the entrance. Workers in Car 'n Suds uniforms stand by huge vacuum cleaners. The picture makes me nervous. The people in it look like they could be from El Salvador. I pass it to LaShaunda.

"The baby has to go back, too?" LaShaunda asks.

"No," Sarah says. "The baby was born here so she can stay."

"Who will take care of the baby, Mr. Sandowski?" asks LaShaunda.

"It's a complicated situation," Mr. Sandowski says.

"Hey, pass that over here," Randall says. "I want to see it."

LaShaunda hands the paper to Randall.

"My father says people like this should go back to their own countries," says Randall. "We didn't ask them to come here. They took their chances."

Some didn't have any choice, I want to say, but keep quiet.

"Randall," Mr. Sandowski says, "there are some laws in our country that do not seem fair to everyone. What if we send people back to a country where we know their lives are in danger? Then do you think it's right to send them back?"

"Well, if it's the law, if they're not supposed to be here," Randall says.

I grasp my hands together tightly under my desk.

"People come to this country for many reasons," Mr. Sandowski says. His voice is high, with that tone he has when he's about to begin a long lesson.

I squeeze my hands. Please stop talking about this, Mr. Sandowski. Please just stop.

"Throughout history, our country has welcomed immigrants to our country for economic, political, and religious reasons. And sometimes," Mr. Sandowski's voice goes on, "when countries are at war …"

My knuckles turn white.

"… people come here seeking asylum. Asylum is when you give people shelter from a dangerous situation. Right now there are countries at war…"

Just then, the lunch bell rings. Lesson over. You can stop talking now, Mr. Sandowski, I think. "All right, then. That's enough for today," Mr. Sandowski says. Kids' chairs start moving, desktops open and close. "Go ahead and line up."

My heart is pounding. What if our papers don't come in time? What if Mamá, Nico, and I get sent back like that man from Guatemala? Would the soldiers who took Papá be waiting for us? Would we be sent to prison? Would we have to hide out in a cave?

After lunch we have social studies. It's my turn to give my report on a famous *norteamericano* from the 1800s. We were supposed to dress up and pretend to be the person. Mr. Sandowski chose an artist, Winslow Homer, for me because he said we both liked to draw. He gave me books to read at home. Mrs. Harrison brought over poster board and markers. She found a straw hat for my costume. I spent forever trying to copy my favorite painting by Homer – a ship at sea. I practiced my talk for Mamá and Nico. Nico had put on the straw hat, too, and Mamá and I laughed when the hat fell below Nico's eyes. I was nervous about the report, but I was pretty sure I was ready.

Until now. Now that I'm making a fool of myself. First, the sheets of poster board start slipping out of my hands. Then, I drop my note cards and watch them scatter on the floor. When I bend over to pick them up, my straw hat falls off. In the back of the room, Randall is laughing.

I jumble my cards back in order, prop the posters against the chalkboard, and start to put the hat back on. This hat is stupid. It's way too big for my head. At home, it seemed like a good idea. Now I wish it would disappear. I put it aside.

"Ready to get started, Mario?" Mr. Sandowski asks.

I'm ready to be invisible, but I turn to face the class. "My name is Winslow Homer," I say. "I was born in …" This is so dumb. I read from my note cards. I tell the story of Winslow Homer's life, where he was born, where he lived, who was in his family.

Then I put down my cards and point to my posters and pictures in the books to talk about the paintings. "Winslow Homer, I mean, *I*, like to paint the sea, men fishing, and stormy waves. See right here? This one's called *The Fog Warning*. See the storm coming in? How the fisherman pulls on his oars? The huge waves? See how he, I mean, I, painted the tips gray and white?" I keep going. I like talking about Homer's paintings and artistic techniques.

"Excellent job, Mario," Mr. Sandowski says when I'm done. "I can tell you put a lot of time into this report. Did you know Winslow Homer also drew illustrations of the Civil War? Did you come across any of those?"

Oh yeah. I saw the illustrations. But I didn't like looking at them. Not at all. The one called *Sharp Shooter on Picket Duty* made me want to rip the page from the library book. A young man was perched in a tree, his rifle balanced on a branch. He was aiming at something. At someone. He was getting ready to fire. I couldn't take my eyes off the tip of the rifle. Where was it pointing? Who was it pointing at? Studying that horrible illustration, I had a vision of Papá's face. I imagined the soldier was taking aim at Papá. I wanted to reach into the picture and turn the rifle away.

"Not really," I say.

Mr. Sandowski explains to the class that Winslow Homer had a job with a magazine to illustrate real scenes from the Civil War. "We didn't have T.V. news then. Homer's illustrations helped people in the north see for themselves what was happening during the war."

I remember what Oscar said, how it was important to write about what happened to Papá. *People should know*, he said.

"Does anyone have questions for Mario?" Mr. Sandowski asks the class.

"Was Winslow Homer a klutz, too?" It's Randall. I see him slouched over his desk, cupping his chin in his hand, with his wise-aleck expression on his face. Some kids start laughing.

"Randall," Mr. Sandowski says in his warning voice.

"At least he was American," Randall says.

"That's enough," Mr. Sandowski says.

I go back to my desk and bump against Randall's chair. "Shut up, Randall," I say.

Randall bends forward. "I have the video now, you know," he says. "So, you're the one who should shut up, Punk-Face."

"Who'd like to go next?" Mr. Sandowski asks.

A girl named Monica raises her hand and goes to the front of the room. The class talks quietly while she arranges her posters and props.

Mr. Sandowski asks the class to settle down: Monica's ready to give her report. She's Harriet Beecher Stowe. She sets up a desk at the front of the room and talks about <u>Uncle Tom's Cabin</u>, the book she's 'writing.' She holds up a quill pen and says something about it being "authentic."

I'm not really listening. All I can think about is Randall and the tape and how he could easily hand it over to the police. From now on, I'm going to be extra careful. I'm going to stay away from Randall. Go straight home after school. And never leave the apartment again.

18

FROM THE FISH'S EYE

I t's a good thing I told LaShaunda and William I couldn't go to the park because that afternoon, Mamá comes home early from work with Nico.

"We're going to the park, Mario," she says. "For a picnic supper. It's such a beautiful day."

Outside the pink flowers have bloomed on the magnolia trees. A warm breeze sends their sweet smell through the opened windows. Mamá hums as she makes sandwiches and packs them in her bag. I haven't heard Mamá hum in a long time.

"I have news," Mamá says, her eyes sparkling, as they walk.

"What kind of news?" I ask.

"News from home, Mario! I talked to Nicolás."

"Tío Nicolás? Can he come here?" Nico asks.

"Is Mrs. Harrison going to help him, too?" I ask.

"Ay, *niños*. One question at a time," Mamá says, smiling. She explains that Nicolás contacted newspaper reporters in New York about covering our story. Someone has taken an interest and is working to get him out of the country.

"Would Tío come here?" I ask.

"We must pray for it, Mario," she says.

"Tío would live with us?" I ask.

Mamá stops walking. She takes my hand and squeezes it. She looks me in the eyes. "Yes, Mario, if everything works out," she says, her voice soft, her eyes full of hope. "I don't have to tell you, Mario, that while these negotiations are going on, we have to be careful. We can't draw attention to ourselves. Word could get back. If the people who took Papá…" Mamá says. She swallows hard. "If they find out about the plans, they could stop our Nicolás."

Mamá continues talking. If the authorities find Nicolás. If they think Nicolás is trying to flee the country. If they find out where we're living. If we get sent back.

Mamá's voice travels in my ears as if echoing down a dark tunnel. I understand the words. But all I can see is the image of a hand, my hand, reaching for candy bars and jamming them in my pocket, on Randall's video.

"We need something to drink for our picnic," Mamá says. "Let's stop at that store on the corner."

Oh great. JP's Variety.

"Come. Show me what drink you like," she says, wrapping her arm around my shoulder.

I go straight to the cooler. I pick out a lemonade and glance up at the camera. It makes a sweep of the entire store, including the candy counter. I look in the round reflector mirror. Staring right at me, out of the fish eye, is Randall.

Up front, Randall's unpacking bags of chips and putting them in a rack. His father stands behind the cash register. "How's it going, Mario?" Randall asks when we come to pay for the drinks.

Mamá's taking forever, fumbling with her wallet, looking for the right change. Doesn't she understand the coins yet? Can't she hurry up?

"No candy today?" Randall asks.

"Mamá, can we get candy?" Nico asks. "Please?"

Randall says, "Doesn't your brother want a Sky Bar?"

"A Sky Bar? What's that?" Nico asks.

I grab Nico's arm. As I pull him to the door, I look back at the video camera. Now Randall had a recording of Mamá and Nico on his tape, too.

19

"I have the perfect job for you," Mr. Sandowski tells me. Our class is in the school's auditorium. We're spending the afternoon working on the fifth grade play. The play is about a slave who escapes on the underground railway. At one end of the room, kids have cans of paint and are painting trees. Next to them is a huge cardboard box, the kind refrigerators come in.

"That's what I thought you could work on, Mario," Mr. Sandowski says, pointing to the box. "It's going to be the tower. We'll cut off the back section and make a hole for the window. The person who's playing the captured slave can enter from the back. You could paint stones and ivy. Make it look real."

I look at box. There are also scraps of brown paper left over from the scenery the other kids are painting. I get an idea. "Can I add a twisting vine?" I ask.

"You're the artist. Paint anything you like," Mr. Sandowski says.

"No, I mean, we could use this brown paper. Roll it into branches then twist them to look like wood," I say.

"I knew I had the right man for the job," Mr. Sandowski says. He pats me on the back.

"And we can glue paper leaves to the vine," I say.

"Another great Mario idea!" The way Mr. Sandowski says 'Mario idea' reminds me of when Papá used to with sit with me to look at my school papers or my drawings. It's a nice memory and it surrounds me when I'm rolling tubes of brown paper and twisting them into vines. I'm not thinking about anything, not Randall or the tape or Tío Nicolás. For a second, I let myself pretend that Papá's looking over me, watching me with my new friends, as we make scenery for the play.

Next come the leaves from construction paper. I cut them with scissors and carefully glue them to the vines. Mr. Sandowski comes to look at the tower. The box is nearly covered with the paper bag vines, but I still have a pile left on the floor. "This looks terrific, Mario," he says. "Randall, come help Mario finish up."

Randall? Why, Randall, Mr. Sandowski? I keep my eyes on my work.

Randall kicks the vines lying on the floor. He tugs at a vine on the tower.

"What are you doing?" I ask. I was so careful when I attached them. I rolled each piece of masking tape so the audience couldn't see it. Randall pulls off a vine. "Stop it," I say.

"What are you going to do about it, Punk-Face, call the police?" Randall laughs meanly and pulls off one vine, then another, and another. "I'm not working on any dumb baby cardboard tower with *you*," Randall says, kicking the edge of the box. He takes a quick look at the stage to make sure Mr. Sandowski isn't watching, and sneaks out of the room.

The torn branches are all around me on the floor. Slowly, I begin to twist them back into shape and attach new pieces of masking tape. If only I could get Mr. Sandowski over here, tell him what happened, get Randall in trouble. Get Randall thrown out of school, I think, as I tear off new pieces of tape. Get Randall sent to another city. No, get Randall sent to El Salvador and let the soldiers have at him.

But I can't do that. I have to do whatever anyone in this country tells me. Stay in the apartment. Go to meetings with Mamá and Mrs. Harrison. Be good in school. Keep quiet so Randall won't show the tape to the police.

On the stage, kids are setting out the props, testing the pulls on the curtain. At the back of the room, William's playing around with the spotlight, trying to center it on the stage. LaShaunda's jumping and darting in and out of the spotlight, making faces at William. The kids love doing this play. They've been working on it for weeks. They think my tower is great. I pick up a vine and press it to the box.

Mr. Sandowski comes over. "What happened here?" he asks. "Where's Randall?"

I shrug.

"And the vines?" Mr. Sandowski asks.

"I'm doing them over. I didn't put on the right kind of tape," I say. I don't look at Mr. Sandowski when I speak. I just keep working. If I tell Mr. Sandowski the truth, there's no telling what Randall will do to me and my family.

That night, I toss and turn and can't fall asleep. I'm wide awake, staring at the changing shapes of shadow and light on the ceiling. Cars move on the street, their headlights becoming brighter as they approach, then fading as they pass by. I try to concentrate on the patterns, and stop worrying about Randall and what he might do next. But I keep seeing my tower destroyed and the nasty, twisted expression on Randall's face.

I click on the light and reach for my notebook and pencils. I skip the pages with Papá's letter. I find a blank page and draw a picture of Randall, surrounded by paper vines scattered all over the floor.

20

Mr. Sandowski has divided the class into pairs to work on a project. We're supposed to draw a map of the school neighborhood. I'm working with LaShaunda. First we made rough sketches on scrap paper. Now we're copying the maps on poster board. LaShaunda draws the lines for the streets and writes their names. When she's done with a section, she turns the poster board in my direction and I make illustrations of the school, the park, the row of stores in the small shopping area. Mr. Sandowski has music playing for us to listen to while we work.

Sarah looks over to see what we're doing. "Wow, Mario you're a really good artist," she says.

"You even drew the soccer field?" William asks.

Other kids come over and point out where they live. They tell me what their houses look like so I can draw them, too.

Randall stands over the map. "I don't see my father's store," he says.

"So?" LaShaunda says.

"Now, how could you go and forget JP's Variety? When Mario's one of our most famous customers?"

"Randall, what are you talking about?" LaShaunda asks.

"Mario knows what I'm talking about," Randall says.

"Nothing. It's nothing," I say. But I draw in the store all the same.

When I leave school that day, Randall pushes me out of line. He's tossing something in the air and catching it. It's Rana, Nico's frog! "Hey, that belongs to my brother," I shout.

"It's mine now," Randall says. "And if you say anything to Mr. Sandowski, that video goes straight to the police."

That night when Mamá comes home from work with Nico, she's got a shoebox filled with toys from one of the families she works for. "Look, Mario. A whole box of cars!" Nico cries, reaching up to take the box from Mamá. He lifts off the lid, and a dozen little racecars spill out all over the floor.

"Come on, Mario. Let's play," Nico says.

I get down on the floor to keep Nico entertained while Mamá makes dinner. The cans of soup are gone now. Mamá is cooking a pot of chicken and rice, just the way Blanca used to. As we line up all the cars in a row, I think about the frog Papá made for Nico. How Randall has it now. It kills me to think of Rana anywhere near Randall. I vow to get him back for my little brother.

"Let me hear you count, Nico," I say.

"One, two, tree, five, six, seven…" Nico counts.

I laugh. "Try again. Say after me: one, two, three, four…" We count fourteen cars all together, and something tickles the back of my mind. Didn't I grab cars off my table in El Salvador? They must still be in the bag I shoved into Mamá's closet when we first got here. "I'll be right back," I tell Nico.

I go to Mamá's room and look in the closet. I find the bag hanging on a hook behind Mamá's clothes. I get it down and dig around for the cars. They're not in the big compartment. I unzip a side pocket. Not there. I try the other side. I reach in and feel a crumpled up sheet of paper.

Papá's article. The one I pulled from the typewriter that night. I take out the paper and unfold it. Sitting on Mamá's bed, I read.

> Today my ten-year-old son came home full of fear and rage. Two soldiers had stopped him on his way home from school. "Why, do they have to bother us?" he asked me. "We're only kids. We have nothing to do with the war. Why does there even have to be a war?"

What simple answer could I give to my ten-year-old boy? That while most of our people live in poverty, it is only a few families who control the government and own the land? That our government has an army that uses death squads and intimidation? That thousands of civilians who have no involvement in the war have been tortured and killed? Should I tell my son about the farmer with five small children who was shot for giving food to the rebels? Or about the peasants 'let go' by their landlords only to starve to death near the fields they once tended? How about our university's president, shot in his office by guerillas?

How can I pass this world on to my son? Some would have me sit quietly and wait for the war to pass. Play it safe, they say. There is no playing safe in time of war. How can I shield my eyes and keep silent when I know that all over our country there are fathers like me who are helpless to protect their children?

No one is safe from the madness. But there is great determination among our people. We must stay strong, keep our faith, and continue to seek justice. We must arm ourselves with ideals, not weapons. We must tell the truth to sow

seeds for peace. We must do it for our
children. I must do it for my sons.

The article ends. The crumpled paper shakes in my
hands. I read it again and I'm sent back in time. I am
with Papá, looking over his shoulder as he writes. I see
his fingers tap and dance over the typewriter keys. I
see him stop and pull his hands through his hair. I
hear him groan in frustration. I watch him straighten
in his chair and start typing again furiously. My world
stops. Papá's words crawl into me and settle.

"Mario," Nico calls. "Where are you? Are you coming?"

Papá's last article was about me.

"Mario!" Nico yells. "Aren't you going to play with me?"

When the soldiers came, Papá made sure that I got
it from his typewriter.

Nico comes in to Mamá's room and tugs at my
shirt. "Come on!"

I fold Papá's article carefully and slip it back into
the bag. I find my old racecars in another pocket. I let
Nico take my hand and pull me into the living room.

Papá wanted me to know: he loved me and he loved
his country. Papá wanted to protect me and make the
world a better place for me. He never wanted to hurt me.

Nico takes the racecars from my hand. "Where'd
you get these?" he asks, lining them up with the others.

"Those cars?" I say. "They're very special. They
came all the way from home."

21

CURTAIN!

I t's Saturday, the day of the play. I'm standing on stage, hidden behind the curtains. Mr. Sandowski gave me the job of opening and closing the curtains. Randall's on the other side of the stage. His job is to move out props or take things from the actors as they come off the stage. He's holding on to a pair of candlesticks for the first scene, firing them, pretending they're guns. He aims at LaShaunda and laughs. He thinks he's being funny. LaShaunda doesn't even notice.

I peek through a slit in the curtains and watch as people enter the auditorium and find seats. Everyone's talking. Mr. Sandowski is hushing the kids behind stage. I check the ropes on the curtains and remind myself to move my hands one above the other so the curtains open smoothly. Soon, William dims the lights and the audience is quiet. The actors take their places on stage.

Mr. Sandowski crouches down at the front. Waving his arm with a gesture like an orchestra conductor that says *one-two-ready-go*! he hits the button on the tape player and music fills the room.

I pull the curtains open. I squint my eyes in the bright light to peer out at the audience. Mamá's sitting with Nico at the end of a row. Two rows behind Mamá, is Randall's father. Does he recognize Mamá? Is he watching her?

William shines the spotlight on LaShaunda, and the show begins.

In the second-to-last scene, I stand poised to close the curtain. We rehearsed the scene many times and I'm ready for my cue. The runaway slave is hiding in the tower. The lighting is muted: it's nighttime on stage. A paper moon hangs in the sky. Mr. Sandowski called this a dramatic moment. We have to get it just right. Mr. Sandowski plays a tape of crickets and night sounds.

From stage right, the bounty hunters enter, searching for the escaped slave. Their heavy oversized boots clomp loudly. My eyes are drawn to their feet as they tramp across the stage. Like sparks, the lights are reflected in the polished leather. Clomp, clomp, clomp, they march. In rehearsals, they never marched so loudly. Clomp, clomp, clomp, CLOMP!

The noise echoes in my ears. I look down to the audience, to Mamá's huddled shape, dark now in the unlit auditorium. The hunters come closer to the tower. They beat on the side. Back stage, Randall bangs a stick on the floor to make the noise louder. Thump, thump, THUMP!

"Aieeeeee," the slave screams. Then the stage goes black. This is my cue. I'm supposed to pull the curtain when the lights go out.

Instead, I freeze.

"Curtain!" Randall cries in a stage whisper.

But I'm back in my old house in El Salvador. It's the soldiers, not the bounty hunters, who are coming. Papá's clicking on his typewriter. They're coming for Papá. Clomp, clomp, CLOMP! I heard the soldiers. Why didn't I do anything? Why didn't I run to Papá? Why didn't I push him into another room, out the back door?

"Mario! Curtain!" comes another voice.

Into a closet. Anywhere. I heard them coming. I could've done something. Why did I just stand by?

Randall's beside me. He grabs the cord out my hands, yanks it, and the curtains close. "What's wrong with you, Punk-Face? That was your cue, remember? *You* were supposed to close the curtain," he says.

The audience starts clapping. The actors leave the stage. Randall runs back to the center, removes the tower, and puts a table and chairs at center stage for the last scene.

"Am I going to have to open it for you, too?" Randall asks when he comes back.

"I can do it," I say. My head is spinning. I'm caught in a dream, a nightmare. There's pressure behind my ears. Nothing sounds right.

The actors are ready for the next scene. Randall nudges me. "Curtain!" he says. I open the curtain. Then Randall drags me off to the side. "What's wrong with you anyway?" he whispers.

"My father." My voice is soft, like I'm speaking in a trance.

"Your father? What are you talking about?"

"Soldiers came. They took him. They took Papá. They killed him."

"Your father's dead?"

"They threw him in a pile." I can see it. Papá's body is draped over a pile of other bodies. He's in his pajamas.

"Are you crazy?" says Randall.

Suddenly, the fog in my head clears. What am I doing? What am I saying? I'm at the school play. I'm talking to Randall. I look at the actors on the stage. We're in the middle of scene four. I'm supposed to pull the curtain now, aren't I? I go to the rope, reach for it.

"Not now," Randall says.

I glare at him.

"Your father. He did something bad? Is that why you came here?" he asks.

Papá? Bad? Is that what people think? That we had to come to this country because Papá did something bad? I think of Papá's article and all the others that must have come before it. "No, Randall," I say. "We came here because my father, he did something great."

22

PAPÁ'S LETTER

Later, after Mamá and Nico go to sleep, I turn on my light and sit up on the couch. I have been thinking about this all afternoon, during the applause, over refreshments, while striking down the set and cleaning up. I take out the notebook. I open to the page with Papá's letter. I stare at writing until it blurs. Please, Papá. Tell me what to do. Tell me what to do about Randall.

I read Papá's letter. This time, I'm going to read it from beginning to end.

> *Dear Mario,*
>
> *If you are reading this letter, it means the soldiers have taken me, and you and Mamá and Nico have fled the country.*
>
> *You must be brave and strong, Mario.*
>
> *Be a good son to Mamá. Help her with Nico so he'll grow up to be a smart boy just*

*like you. Teach Nico to be honest and kind,
and to do good for others as I have tried to
teach you.*

*My son, I know how you must be suffer-
ing. Please don't hold the pain in your heart.
Use this notebook to write to me, Mario. When
you write, pretend I'm here to read what you
say. Writing helps take away the sorrow.*

*Please try to forgive me, and know that
I had no choice for myself or for our country. We can't abandon our ideals or turn our
backs on what we believe in. What kind of life
can a man live who knows the truth but does
not tell it?*

I run my finger along where Papá signed his name.
I take my pen and copy the last line of Papá's letter,
changing one word:

What kind of life can a boy *live who knows
the truth but does not tell it?*

When I finish writing, I picture Papá reading my question. Papá is looking up at me with that quizzical expression of his that says, *Why are you asking me when you
know the answer yourself?* For a second, it's as if Papá's in
the room with me.

I turn the page and start drawing. I draw me, stealing the candy, with the video camera aimed right at

me. I draw Randall surrounded by little kids, Nico's frog in one hand and the sparkly ball in the other. When I'm done, I tear the picture from my notebook. I also tear the one of Randall and the ripped paper vines. I fold the pictures and put them in my backpack.

24

SEEDS OF PEACE

The next day at school, when nobody's looking, I slip the three pictures--me stealing the candy, Randall with Nico's frog, Randall and the ripped paper vines--in Mr. Sandowski's Suggestion Box.

At the end of the school day, Mr. Sandowski asks me to stay back in the classroom and take a seat. He takes out my pictures from his desk drawer.

"Would you like to tell me about these?" he asks.

"What are they?" I ask.

"Nobody draws like you do, Mario," Mr. Sandowski says, smiling.

Mr. Sandowski opens the picture of Randall and the vines. "I can see the message in this one, but I'm curious about the other drawing."

Right now I wish I'd never drawn the pictures. What was I thinking?

"What's going on, Mario?" Mr. Sandowski asks in a very soft voice. "Is there something you want to tell me?"

The nice way Mr. Sandowski is talking to me makes my head throb at the temples. If I don't get up fast, I'm going to start crying right here. In front of my teacher! I walk away and stare at the fish in the tank. I think about Randall tearing up the paper vines. I'm thinking about Randall stealing from the little kids. I picture Randall watching the video tape at home, gloating, glowering, making his plans.

I take a pinch of fish food and sprinkle it in the tank. All at once the hungry fish dart to the surface. So do my words. "I'm not allowed to leave my apartment after school. Mamá says it's dangerous. But LaShaunda and William were right there. They got me a bike." I keep talking. I'm telling Mr. Sandowski all about leaving the apartment when I shouldn't, going to the park, stealing the Sky Bars, getting caught. "If Mamá ever finds out... I'm supposed to help Mamá, not cause more problems. I took the candy back, Mr. Sandowski. I promise I did. But Randall has me on a videotape. Mamá, too. He said if I don't watch out, he's going to give that tape to the police. Then Uncle Nicolás will never get out of El Salvador. He'll be murdered. Just like Papá. And it'll be my fault."

"Whoa," Mr. Sandowski says. "Slow down a second, Mario. Come sit here." He brings a cup of water. "Drink this."

I take a sip.

"Your fault?" Mr. Sandowski asks.

"When the soldiers came for Papá," I say, "one of them, I'd seen before. I should've stayed in Señor Perez's car. I shouldn't have told them my name. I should've warned Papá. Then none of this would have happened." I'm crying now and I don't care.

"Mario," Mr. Sandowski says. "No one could've stopped the soldiers."

"I could have. I heard them coming. I could have…"

"No you couldn't," Mr. Sandowski says. "No man could've stopped those soldiers. So, how could a ten-year-old boy?"

"But if I had warned Papá, he could've run away," I say.

"And then what?" Mr. Sandowski asks.

"He could hide. He could go to my grandfather's and hide. He could leave the country. He could've come here."

"Mario, I've heard about Joaquín Zamora. He was not a man to hide. He had too many more words to write to help end the war."

Papá and his late nights. The worried conversations with people who came by. How worked up he got when he heard about the killings and destruction. I think about what Papá wrote in his last article: *We must tell the truth to sow seeds for peace.*

"Do you really think your father would ever give up?" Mr. Sandowski asks.

Mr. Sandowski is right. Papá would've never given up until the war was over.

"What about Randall and the tape?" I ask.

"First of all, no one's going to tell your mother anything. Some day you might want to, and I promise you, she'll understand. The principal and I have a number of things to talk about with Randall and his family."

"What about my brother's frog?"

"And all the little kids will get their things back."

That night, I ask Nico to come sit with me on the couch.

"What story are we going to read?" Nico asks.

"No story tonight," I say. I open the notebook. "Listen, Nico," I say. "I'm going to read you something from Papá."

I read all of Papá's letter out loud. I know Nico doesn't really understand it, but I'm reading it anyway. Nico won't remember much about Papá, but I'm going to tell him everything. Every day, I'll tell Nico something about our Papá and what a great man he was and how he loved his family and his country. Mamá comes over and sits with us. Her eyes glisten with tears, but she's smiling a little bit, too.

While Mamá puts Nico to bed, there's one more thing I have to do. I take out my drawing pencils. I draw a picture of a man, hunched over his desk, a page of writing in his typewriter. Two soldiers aim rifles at the man. In the shadows, a frightened boy hovers against the wall.

This isn't exactly what happened that night when the soldiers came for Papá. But I want my picture to show what that night felt like to me, then and now. And I want to show Papá writing, not with his hands tied behind his back.

I write a title across the top of his drawing: 'My Father's Last Truth.' I tear the picture from my notebook and put it in an envelope. I get Papá's article from his bag and put it in the envelope, too. Tomorrow I'll ask Mr. Sandowski for help to send both the picture and the article to the *New York Times*.

And then I open my notebook and turn to a fresh, new page.

Dear Papá, I begin.

AUTHOR'S NOTE

I was inspired to write Mario's Notebook in the 1980s during the time of the civil war in El Salvador. I was then a young Spanish bilingual elementary school teacher living in Cincinnati, Ohio. During that time I also hosted a Spanish radio program on community radio station WAIF. Many people from the Hispanic community in Cincinnati, including several families from El Salvador, tuned in and were guests on my weekly program, *Arroz con Leche*. Through them, I learned about the Salvadoran Civil War, their experiences coming to the U.S., and the stories of those they left behind.

I wondered then what it must be like for children to leave behind family and friends during the war. Though Mario's story began churning in my imagination way back then, it took many, many years to write.

I'd never been to El Salvador and knew little of its history so I had to do extensive research including using primary sources in Spanish. I had to learn how to write a novel. As a teacher and mother of two children, it was difficult to find time to write.

But I stuck with it because the deeper I got into my research, the more my heart grew with stories of refugees in our country, the more I needed to tell Mario's story.

With all that's happening in our world today, I believe that Mario's story as a child who has to leave his country because of war and become a refugee in the U.S. is an important one that, unfortunately, many such children and their caregivers will relate to.

ACKNOWLEDGMENTS

Because *Mario's Notebook* was a work-in-progress for so many years, there were a lot of people who helped me. In the book's early stages, members of my critique group back then—Jacqueline Davies, Tracey Fern, Sarah Lamstein, and Carol Peacock—read early drafts and helped me along the way. When I started submitting the manuscript to publishers, some editors worked with me and encouraged me to keep going. To all editors who take the time to guide an author with personal correspondence, thank you. I'd like to especially thank Abby Ranger for her editorial expertise and ongoing interest in Mario's story. Special thanks also go to Alba Azucena Lopez, consul general of El Salvador in Boston, for taking the time to read and comment on Mario's Notebook. *Muchísmias gracias* to René Colato Laínez for multiple readings of *Mario's Notebook*, his support of the book, and helping me get some details just right. And Elizabeth Gomez, your cover illustration is perfect.

ABOUT THE AUTHOR

Mary Atkinson is the author of *Owl Girl* and *Tillie Heart and Soul*. Her poetry for children has appeared in magazines and anthologies, and her fiction and nonfiction have been published widely in educational markets. She lives in Maine with her husband Steve and dog Maisie. For more on the author, visit www.maryatkinson.net.

90740532R00074

Made in the USA
Columbia, SC
11 March 2018